TO THE VICTOR BELONGS THE SPOILS

Judith was still breathing hard when Zach dismounted and came to her, reaching his hands up to her waist to help her from the saddle.

"First," she said, putting her hands on his wrists to stop him from lifting her down, "tell me what I am to forfeit. What will you seek in payment for your triumph?"

Zach stood quite still, his hands almost circling her slim waist, and looked up into her gamine face. Her usually neat hair was in glorious disarray, the medium-brown tresses wind-tossed and falling all about her shoulders, and her eyes were bright with the excitement of the race. Her soft, full lips were slightly parted and Zach knew without question what he meant to collect as his reward.

"I am tempted," he said, "to take my 'winnings' from your lips."

A quick, nearly inaudible gasp was her only response.

"A kiss," he said softly. "A small forfeiture, surely, for one who bade me name my own prize."

He gave her several moments to say him nay, if that was her wish, but she said nothing. She merely stared at him, and though her big blue eyes exhibited uncertainty, they showed neither fright nor refusal.

When Judith felt Zach begin to lift her slowly from the saddle, she leaned toward him, resting her hands upon his upper arms, an action that put their faces mere inches apart . . .

ROMANCE FROM JANELLE TAYLOR

ANYTHING FOR LOVE   (0-8217-4992-7, $5.99)

DESTINY MINE   (0-8217-5185-9, $5.99)

CHASE THE WIND   (0-8217-4740-1, $5.99)

MIDNIGHT SECRETS   (0-8217-5280-4, $5.99)

MOONBEAMS AND MAGIC   (0-8217-0184-4, $5.99)

SWEET SAVAGE HEART   (0-8217-5276-6, $5.99)

THE GALLANT GAMBLER

Martha Kirkland

Zebra Books
Kensington Publishing Corp.
http://www.zebrabooks.com

ZEBRA BOOKS are published by

Kensington Publishing Corp.
850 Third Avenue
New York, NY 10022

Zebra and the Z logo Reg. U.S. Pat. & TM Off.

First Printing: June, 1997
10 9 8 7 6 5 4 3 2 1

Printed in the United States of America

For Marcia and Arthur Deitt,
and for two women who prove that childhood
friendships can be sustained through the years,
Martha Porter Hall and Marilyn Riley Harris.

One

Dorset, May 1819

"Lilia shall not marry him!"

Outraged, Miss Judith Preston pushed aside the brace of work candles that stood in the middle of the small mahogany table, the better to look into her mother's suddenly pale face. "Tell him, Mama. Inform Lord Gillmore that he has no right to expect Lilia to do his bidding."

Dorothy Gillmore did not acquiesce to her daughter's wishes. She could not, no matter how much she might wish to do so. The middle-aged lady, still attired in her widow's black, licked her suddenly dry lips, but said nothing to the elderly gentleman who sat on the opposite side of the drawing room from her and her oldest daughter. After sending Judith a pleading look—a look that begged her not to anger the man in whose house they now resided—Mrs. Gillmore returned her gaze to the needlepoint square she held in her hands.

Though Judith understood all too well the reason for her mother's silent plea, she refused to stand by idly while the old tyrant ran roughshod over their lives. "Mama, please. You must not allow his lordship to bully you. What he suggests is out of the question."

When her mother remained silent, Judith tossed the dog-eared book of sonnets she had been perusing onto the polished surface of the table. "Is it not enough that we bow to his lordship's every whim just to keep a roof over our heads and food in our mouths? Must we now allow him to dictate our futures as well?"

Hearing the imperious thump of the old gentleman's cane upon the etched tiles of the hearth, the young lady glanced across the room to the fire whose orange and yellow flames burned brightly beneath the slate mantelpiece. A leather wing chair was drawn quite close to the hearth, yet the occupant of the chair seemed to find no pleasure in the warmth. At the moment, cold fury caused his thick, iron-gray eyebrows to meet above the bridge of his hawk-like nose.

" 'Tis not to be marveled at," Judith said, "that my sister has taken to her bed with the headache."

"Hold your tongue, missy!" Lord Gillmore ordered, glaring at the young woman who never failed to irritate him. He felt no compunctions about doing battle with the insolent creature, not at all misled by Judith's sylphlike appearance or the large blue eyes that gave her slender face its gamine look.

"My granddaughter will do as she is told," he said. "As for you, I will thank you to keep your opinions to yourself, and allow me to attend to those matters pertaining to my family."

"Judith," her mother whispered, "I beg of you, do not cause a scene."

Placing her needlepoint upon the table next to her daughter's book, Dorothy Gillmore took a fortifying breath, then turned, albeit reluctantly, toward her father-in-law. "My lord," she said, "surely this conversation is ill-timed. We know nothing of the future heir, except that he is to arrive on the morrow. It may transpire that the gentleman is already married. Or at the very least, bound to some young lady by a prior promise."

"My mother is right, of course," Judith added. "But even if your heir should prove to be as free as the gulls that soar above the white cliffs at Durdle Door, it would make no difference. Lilia shall not be coerced into taking him."

Lord Gillmore ignored his daughter-in-law's conjecture as to the heir's connubial availability. Instead, he kept his attention riveted upon Judith, the light of battle still shining in his faded brown eyes. "You are an impertinent miss!"

"At least I keep my word! You, my lord, seem to have forgotten the promise you made your only son scarcely a twelvemonth ago. As he drew his last breath, he begged you to take care of my sister and my mother. Is this the way you honor the pledge you made to dear Papa?

"Papa?" Lord Gillmore repeated.

He leaned forward in his chair, a sneer upon his gaunt face. "I made no promises to *your* papa. As a matter of fact, I doubt I laid eyes upon that rakehell above a half-dozen times prior to the fateful day when his debts caught up with him, and he put a pistol to his head."

Judith pressed her lips together to keep them from trembling. This was a familiar weapon, and one the ill-tempered old goat used any time he wished to pierce her armor and go straight for the heart. "Sir. You know quite well that I refer to Papa Albert. I think of your son as my father. I always have and I always will."

"But he was not your father."

"That is true, but when he married my mother, he became my parent in the truest sense of the word. He was the best of men, and in the seventeen years I was fortunate enough to know him, he never once showed a preference for his own daughter over me, always bestowing upon me the same kindness and affection he showed Lilia."

"Humph," was the old gentleman's only reply.

Lord Gillmore stared into the fire for a time, clearing his throat at intervals, and for a few moments Judith felt compassion for him, sorry she had been the cause of his having to deal with his grief in the presence of two women he so patently disliked. However, when he spoke again, his words were more belligerent than before, driving all sympathy from her thoughts.

"If my boy had married the person I chose for him—a young lady of fortune as well as family—instead of aligning himself with a penniless widow five years his senior, he might be sitting beside me this very minute, alive and well. He would still be my heir, and I would not now be forced to confront another."

Dorothy Gillmore gasped; then, her eyes brimming with tears, she fled the room.

"Sir!" Judith said, rising abruptly, and grasping the edge of the table to keep herself from throwing her book at him. "Apparently you have chosen to rewrite such history as pertains to yourself, so I will remind you that it was by your own decree that your son did not set foot in this house for seventeen years. And as for his being alive at this moment, pray remember, sir, that it was a fall from a skittish horse that killed Albert Gillmore, and not marriage to my mother."

Judith turned and crossed the red and blue Axminster carpet, her head held high, her shoulders back. As her hand touched the brass knob of the drawing room door, she turned, facing the lone figure once again.

"You might spare a thought, my lord, for your son's wishes regarding the only child of his flesh and blood. Above all else, he wanted Lilia's happiness. Since he refused to marry a woman of your choosing, I cannot believe he would have stood by and let you coerce his daughter into marrying the future heir. He would not, and believe me, I shall not."

"Be warned," Lord Gillmore said, pointing his cane at her as though it were a sword, "I will brook no interference in my own home. My granddaughter is a biddable girl, and if you say anything to persuade her to defy me, neither you nor your mother will be allowed to remain at Gillmore House. And that is one promise, I assure you, I will keep!"

The handsome chaise and four traveled the final leg of the two-day journey from London to the market town of Blinbourne at a good clip. Earlier, while the two gentlemen had partaken of the hearty breakfast served them at the posting inn in Dorcester, a gentle rain had fallen, but owing to the shower's brief duration, it had not played havoc with the chalky Dorset soil, leaving it in travelable condition.

Now, as the coachman turned the team from the main road onto a narrow lane that sloped sharply upward, Lieutenant Andrew Gillmore was forced to prop one booted foot against the opposite seat to keep from being tossed into the floor of his brother's gold-trimmed maroon traveling coach.

"We must be nearing Gillmore House," Mr. Zachery Camden said once the lane leveled out somewhat and he was able to let go the leather handstraps.

"Let us hope we are near," his brother said, "for the sooner we get there, the sooner the fortnight will end, and I can return to town and to my regiment."

Unaware of the upheaval his anticipated arrival had caused within Lord Gillmore's household—especially among the three females who had resided beneath his lordship's roof for the past year—the future heir yawned. "I cannot tell you how happy I am that you agreed to accompany me, Zach. Bound to be a dreadful bore, don't you know?"

If the truth be told, Mr. Camden sincerely hoped the visit would prove to be a bore. Unfortunately, something—some visceral intuition—told him this would not be the case.

As a result of the untimely demise of Lord Gillmore's son, plus the practice of entailment, Zach's half-brother, Andrew, had become next in line to the barony and the estate. And though a twelvemonth had passed since the funeral of the previous heir, Andrew had received not one word of communication from the present baron. Not, that is, until three days ago, when a letter suddenly arrived from his lordship, asking Lieutenant Gillmore to come to Dorset for a fortnight.

Upon reading the over-solicitous invitation, Zach's intuition told him that something was afoot. Though the writer of the missive mentioned a desire to extend the hand of friendship, Zach was not convinced. Because he had learned years ago to listen to his intuition, he had invited himself to accompany his sibling.

Not that Andrew would be pleased if he knew his older brother had come along merely to protect him. To the contrary. He would be indignant. Nearing twenty-two years of age, the lad considered himself a man of the world, wise to the ways of scoundrels. Zach knew better.

Society—both high and low—was peopled with those who would relieve a man of his purse, his honor, even his freedom, and smile while they accomplished the dirty deed. Instinct told Zach that Lord Gillmore was just such a one. And whatever his lordship's reasons for this sudden about-face in seeking the immediate acquaintance of his future heir, Zach meant to discover them before any harm could be done his brother.

Not wanting Andrew to discern his thoughts, Zach mentally donned that mask his discreditors referred to as his *whist face,* then he leaned forward to look out the window. To his left, the green hills of the downs rose in grassy swells, while to his right, the distant scarps plunged to the Channel below. "What magnificent country," he said. "Molded, no doubt, by nature's sense of drama and adventure."

"Egad!" the younger man said, disgust writ plainly upon his face. "Hope you don't mean to turn poetic on me over a few hills."

Zach chuckled. "Poetry is not in my line, so you may rest easy on that score. However, even you must admit that a man could remain for months at a stretch in such countryside as this without ever wishing to leave."

"I admit no such thing. But I tell you what, if you like the area so much, why do you not lease a place close by? 'Twould make a nice retreat when you grow weary of town. In fact," he added after a moment's reflection, "be happy to rent you Gillmore House, for I certainly have no wish to reside there. Of course, it may be early days for thinking of the estate as mine. After all, who can say how many years the present owner has left in his dish."

"Who, indeed? One should not be misled by the information that Lord Gillmore has celebrated his seventy-fourth birthday, for from what I was able to discover of the man, he is cantankerous enough to outlive Methuselah."

Andrew's dark blond eyebrows lifted in surprise. "You don't say so. Don't believe I would care to live for hundreds of years. Nevertheless, if that is the old gentleman's goal, I wish him long life and continued joy of his home and his title.

"And that being said," he continued, "what say you to my instructing the coachman to wheelabout this instant and return us to town? I could be back in time for the Colonel's birthday dinner on Friday, and you could stop by to see what is happening on 'Change."

He gave his brother a playful poke with the toe of his boot. "You might well have acquired another fortune since we left. Not that you need it. Like taking coals to Newcastle, don't you know."

Zach smiled, for his brother often teased him about his luck on The Exchange. "Money is but a tool. A man can—"

"I know, I know," Andrew interrupted, then he *sing-songed,* "a man can wear but one pair of boots at a time."

Hearing the repetition of a remark he had made only that morning, Zach laughed. "Your pardon, Lieutenant Gillmore. Obviously, it is *I* who have become a dead bore."

Andrew repudiated the statement; then, reminded of something he had overheard that morning while awaiting his breakfast, he told his brother of the two blacklegs he had seen at the inn.

"I tell you, Zach, I never saw such a pair. One put me in mind of a balding gnome, while the other was built like a prizefighter, his neck the size of an ox's. From the snatches of conversation I heard, there could be no doubt they were 'legs,' for they had come down to take a look at the horses entered in a race meet to be held somewhere in the vicinity. I did not hear the exact date the race was to be held, but it was some time in the near future. I think I'll ask the old gentleman if he knows anything of it. If I am in luck, the meet might be held close enough to Gillmore House for us to have a look in."

While Andrew spoke at length upon the subject of horses and racing, Zach studied his brother's handsome face. He and Andrew were so dissimilar. There was a family resemblance, of course—a certain squareness of the jaw, the same gray eyes—but his half-brother's hair was dark blond, while Zach's was black as a moonless night. As well, the younger man was of slight build—no more than ten stone, compared to Zach's twelve.

More telling, of course, were the differences in their personalities. Andrew's was an open, uncomplicated nature. Fun-loving and gregarious, he was a favorite with all his fellow officers, as well as with the young ladies.

As for Zach, his disposition was far less amiable.

Long before his thirtieth birthday, Zach had amassed a fortune—a circumstance that seemed to bring alleged admirers crawling from out of the woodwork—and though he was respected by his servants, and alternately admired and feared by his colleagues, not one of those people would call him easy to know. Even his brother, the one person he loved, and who loved him, was not privy to his innermost thoughts.

Realizing that Andrew had paused in his monologue, Zach took the opportunity to return to the subject of the Gillmore estate. "Are you not at all curious to see the house and lands you will one day inherit?"

Andrew sighed. "I daresay one *must* be interested. But damnation! I am a soldier. What do I know of collecting the rents, or harvesting corn, and the like?"

"Perhaps," Zach said quietly, "that is the very purpose for which Lord Gillmore has summoned you. To acquaint you with some of the responsibilities of a landowner."

The young gentleman seemed much struck by the idea. "Do you think so?"

Pausing but a moment, Zach replied, "What other reason could he have?"

The cryptic reply fell upon deaf ears, for a sudden disturbance outside the coach caught the passengers' attention. The driver had reined in the horses beside a wooden fence of open palings, and he was yelling something to an old man in a straw hat and workman's smock. As Zach watched, the old man nodded his head, doffed his hat, then walked over to open the wrought-iron gates that bisected the fence.

Shouting his thanks, the coachman gave the four job horses the go-ahead, turning them onto a gravel sweep that curved around a grove of mature silver birches—trees whose smooth white bark was dotted with black diamonds, and whose newly unfurled leaves were green as emeralds. Holding the team to a decorous pace, he continued onward through the spacious hillside park, until he drew up before an Elizabethan mansion.

Long the home of the barons Gillmore, the E-shaped building was not unhandsome, though Zach would have found it more aesthetically pleasing if some recent owner had not seen fit to cover the original stone with painted stucco. In places, the newer facade had fallen away in large chunks, revealing the older, and more attractive silvery gray stone.

"Not too bad," Zach said.

The first to step from the coach, he turned to his brother, who was busy gathering his hat and gloves. "From what I had heard of the present baron's parsimony, I was prepared for much worse. Since his lordship has seen fit to keep the place in fairly good repair, it should not be too expensive to bring it into shape. I wager you will—"

"So," said an apparition who seemed to appear out of thin air, "you are a wagering man."

Startled, Zach turned to stare at a young woman who stood near the corner of the house, practically hidden by an overgrown, pink-blossomed hawthorn bush. She stepped from behind the bush, but when she made no effort to approach him, or to introduce herself, Zach followed suit, remaining where he was, though he let his gaze travel over her slender person. After a cursory inspection of her reed-thin figure, he returned his attention to the large, doe-shaped eyes that stared back at him, looking for all the world as though they belonged in the face of some woodland creature.

She seemed quite otherworldly, yet as he looked her over again, from the shallow-poke straw bonnet that did not quite conceal her dark hair, down to her muddied half-boots, he realized this was no forest nymph who had lost her way. She was a flesh and blood woman, and if the sparks coming from those medium blue orbs was anything to go by, she was also an angry one.

Taller than was considered fashionable, though still much shorter than Zach's six feet, she wore a pale apricot pelisse that suited her clear ivory complexion. When he continued to stare at her, however, the ivory turned to rose, as embarrassment crept into her cheeks. Though not beautiful in the ordinary sense, she was definitely interesting.

Judith felt heat suffuse her face, but she stood her ground, giving this gray-eyed stranger stare for stare, determined not to let him make her look away in confusion. She knew his type. Had she not seen enough of them six years ago, during her come-out? Suave. Devilishly handsome. Immaculately tailored. And so bored by idleness that they thought nothing of risking entire fortunes on the turn of a single card.

A gambler! The very thought made her shudder. The first words out of his mouth once he stepped down from the carriage had been a wager. It wanted only for him to prove a libertine, and her dislike of him would be complete.

And this was the man Lord Gillmore wanted her sister to marry. The future heir! Though there was nothing Judith could do to prevent him from being next in line to Lilia's grandfather, she would not stand by and see her innocent sister sacrificed to this . . . this *rogue!*

"I will not allow it," she muttered.

"Certainly not," he replied, as though they were engaged in conversation.

"No," she said, "you will not do at all."

The fellow had the audacity to smile. If one could call the gesture such, for it was little more than a slow, mocking tug at the corners of his mouth. "Not in the least?"

"You heard me, sir. You will not do for Lilia. And lest you doubt my resolve in this matter, allow me to inform you that I will not let her be badgered into marrying you."

For just an instant something stirred in the man's cool gray eyes, but whatever the emotion, he concealed it immediately, his entire demeanor becoming unreadable, as though he had donned a mask to keep her from looking inside him. "You put my mind at ease, ma'am, for I assure you I have no wish to marry anyone."

He made her a bow gallant enough for a ballroom. "And since I am just as determined not to marry . . . Miss Lilia, was it? . . . as you are to keep my ring from her finger, allow me to thank you from the bottom of my heart for giving me your word that it will not happen. You cannot know what a relief it is to me to know that I have a champion in the house."

Judith had the uncomfortable suspicion that he was making a May game of her, for if there was one thing this tall, muscular fellow did not need, it was someone to defend him. "Make sport of me if you wish, sir, but I am in earnest. My sister shall not—"

"Blast it all, Zach," came a voice from inside the coach, "stand away from the door. I should like to quit the carriage before I am very much older."

After giving Judith a measuring look, one she felt might almost have been a warning, the tall, dark-haired man stepped away from the chaise, allowing the other passenger to alight. The instant the second gentleman's feet touched the gravel, that mocking smile was back upon the face of the rogue.

"Andrew," he said, catching the younger man's arm and propelling him toward Judith, "unless I am very much mistaken, this young lady has something she wishes to say to you."

Judith stared at the gentleman in the Hussar's uniform, searching the open, boyish face, which was the very antithesis of the other man's inscrutable countenance. Instantly realizing that she had erred, she longed for the ground to open up and swallow her. She had made a complete fool of herself, and that . . . that *gambler* had let her do so without saying a word to stop her.

Now, as if to rub salt in her wounds, he said, "Madam, allow me to introduce to you Lieutenant Andrew Gillmore."

Lifting one dark eyebrow in a satirical manner that made Judith long to see him lying at the bottom of the cliff at Durdle Door, he added, "This, you may be relieved to discover, is the gentleman you were expecting."

Two

"Welcome, Lieutenant Gillmore," said the elderly butler, an octogenarian who bowed first to Andrew then to Zach. "I am Peasby, sir, and I used to know your father, Mr. James Gillmore, when he was but a lad."

Andrew said all that was proper to the old servant, then he handed his hat and gloves over to the footman summoned by Peasby.

"Charles will fetch your luggage, sir, and take care of the carriage. If you will be so good as to follow me, his lordship has been awaiting your arrival this hour and more."

Ignoring the gentle reprimand in the butler's words, they followed him, at his snail's pace, into a spacious hall. "Please wait here," he said, indicating a pair of rosewood benches that flanked an unlit fireplace, "while I inform his lordship that you have arrived. I shall not be above a minute." After bowing again, he made his way slowly toward one of three doors that led off the room.

The door where the butler knocked was located to the left, the second door was to the right, while the third was to the rear, behind a wide staircase whose stone steps were worn smooth by the comings and goings of generations of Gillmores. Just to the right of the rear door hung an ancient arras whose crimson, blue, and gold threads were so faded as to make the scene undecipherable, yet whose workmanship was exquisite.

It was while Zach approached the arras for a closer look that he overheard the voice raised in anger. "Show young Gillmore in here at once," ordered the speaker. "As for the other one, send him away."

When the butler did not turn to do his master's bidding, but stood in place, shifting his weight from one foot to the next, all the while clearing his throat, a second voice—this one soft and refined—asked, "Did the two gentlemen travel together, Peasby?"

"They did, Mrs. Gillmore."

"If that is the case, my lord, then you cannot refuse to—"

"Blast it, woman! Do not tell me what I can and cannot do."

"Sir, I merely—"

"Who the deuce told the young jackanapes he might bring a guest? I've not yet put my spoon in the wall, and until I have, I will say who is and who is not invited to Gillmore House."

Not wanting to be guilty of eavesdropping, Zach moved away, and though he heard no more, the discussion obviously continued, for it was several minutes before Peasby returned. If nothing else, good manners had prevailed, for the butler asked both gentlemen if they would follow him to the drawing room.

The scowling old gentleman who sat beside the roaring fire came as no surprise to Zach, for his appearance coincided perfectly with his voice. Without rising to greet his guests, or even nodding in their direction, he banged his cane upon the hearth tiles, then used the stick to point at the butler, motioning for the old retainer to be off and shut the door behind him.

The only show of civility came from the middle-aged

lady who sat behind a table bearing a tea tray. "How do you do?" she asked quietly. "I am Dorothy Gillmore."

"Ma'am," Zach replied, making her a bow.

"Your servant," added Lieutenant Gillmore, clicking his heels together in smart, military fashion.

"Please," the lady said, "will you not be seated and allow me to offer you some refreshments?"

Dorothy Gillmore was a handsome woman, despite her black bombazine dress and the accompanying black lace cap that did nothing to enhance her still blond hair and pale complexion, but she was obviously ill at ease, darting occasional glances toward the old martinet who sat beside the fire.

"Gillmore!" bellowed his lordship, "do not stand there like an addlepate. Get your tea and sit down, for I have no intention of inviting a crick in my neck by looking up at you." Apparently considering the amenities at an end, their host instructed his daughter-in-law to pour him another cup of tea.

After the cups were filled, and a plate of Shrewsbury buns passed around, Dorothy Gillmore broke the strained silence by asking the lieutenant if he and his friend had met with pleasant weather on their trip to Blinbourne.

"Your pardon, ma'am, for not making the proper introductions. This gentleman is Zachery Camden, and though he is, in truth, my friend, he is also my older brother."

"Your brother? I do not understand, sir. You are the heir, are you not?"

"Yes, ma'am," Andrew replied, his easy manners allowing him to relax and smile pleasantly at Mrs. Gillmore. "Zach and I are half-brothers, for he is the son of our mother's first husband, while I am the son of her second. My father was James Gillmore, who was Lord Gillmore's first cousin once removed. What that makes his lordship

and me—second cousins, or first cousins twice removed—
I fear I cannot say."

He laughed at his own confusion. "One may be forgiven
for supposing that our family tree must resemble a jigsaw
puzzle. As for you and me, Mrs. Gillmore, I shall not even
try to decipher what our relationship might be."

"On that score, Lieutenant, I am persuaded that ours is
little more than a connection, for—"

"What I should like to know," Lord Gillmore said, interrupting his daughter-in-law without so much as a by
your leave, "is why there is within this family a propensity
for marrying widows. And *older* widows, at that!"

Noticing the lady's indrawn breath, Zach rose from his
chair by the window and took his cup to her to refill. "I
should think, my lord," he said lazily, "that the answer to
your riddle is quite clear. It is the beauty of the ladies.
During her come-out, my mother was known as 'The diamond of diamonds,' and if your daughter-in-law will forgive my impertinence, I dare say the same might have been
said of her."

Though Mrs. Gillmore blushed to the very roots of her
hair, she said nothing, concentrating instead upon pouring
the tea. To Zach's surprise, the sole response to his com-
ment came from the direction of a pair of oak pocket doors
that offered access to a library at the rear of the drawing
room, and even before he turned to look, he recognized the
voice as belonging to the young woman he had met earlier.
Still in her straw bonnet and apricot pelisse, she had lost
none of that *otherworldness* that put Zach in mind of a
forest creature.

"You are correct," the wood nymph said, pinning him
with those large, blue eyes. "Mama was a beauty."

"Was? You will forgive me, ma'am, but I must take ex-

ception to your semantics. I should rather say that your mother *is* a beauty."

"Quite so," agreed Lieutenant Gillmore.

Blushing again, Mrs. Gillmore said, "Lieutenant and Mr. Camden, though I should have liked to make you known to both my daughters, I am afraid my youngest is still in her room, suffering from the headache. In the meantime, allow me to introduce you to Judith, my firstborn."

Zach took his cue from the nymph, and when she curtsied, as though they were meeting for the first time, he bowed. "A pleasure, Miss Gillmore."

"Preston!" his lordship corrected, yelling loud enough to shake the rafters. "That chit is no relative of mine."

At the shouted remark, Judith bit her bottom lip. Though she had grown accustomed to Lord Gillmore's scathing comments, it was mortifying to be repudiated before strangers.

"Your pardon, Miss Preston," Mr. Camden said, inclining his dark head in an abbreviated bow, "for my error. As for you, Lord Gillmore," he added, "pray forgive my insensitivity in having brought to light a lack you must feel every day. I had thought you blessed with two granddaughters when, in fact, you have only the one. My condolences, sir."

The quiet in the room was palpable, and for a moment, no one seemed to breathe. While Judith waited for the explosion that must surely follow such a reproof, she tried to look behind the stranger's unreadable facade.

Why had he chosen to censure Lord Gillmore for his callous behavior? There had to be a reason, but whatever the gentleman's motive, he kept it to himself. His countenance gave away nothing, yet a person had only to look into those cool gray eyes to know their owner lived by his own rules, saying only what he wished to say, and revealing only what he wished to have known.

He was a gambler, and from what Judith knew of such men, they prospered or failed by their ability to read others. Since Mr. Camden appeared prosperous—from the expensive, tassel-fronted Hessians that hugged his well-shaped calves, to the finely woven linen of his cravat—he must have had a pretty fair notion of Lord Gillmore's nature, must have known his lordship would be livid at being called to book for his behavior.

To Judith's surprise, the explosion never came, and what was even more amazing, the person responsible for forestalling it was her mother.

"Judith, my love," the lady said hurriedly, "I am persuaded that our guests must be heartily sick of sitting still after their long journey. Why do you not take them to the picture gallery and show the Lieutenant the portrait of his great-great-grandfather, the fourth Baron Gillmore?"

"A splendid idea," Andrew said, rising quickly from his chair. "I should like to see the old boy. That is, if Miss Preston would not find it a dead bore."

"She will not," replied the damsel's mother, "for she and Lilia are forever up in the gallery. They miss the little sitting room they shared when they were girls, and as a result, they have all but adopted the area as their own private haven."

She turned to her daughter once again. "My dear, do not neglect to show Mr. Camden the Hogarth. I perceive that he is a gentleman of discernment, and as such, he will appreciate the painting's subtleties of line and color."

A gentleman of discernment?

Rendered speechless—first by her mother's having offered a suggestion that ran counter to his lordship's plans, and second by the shy lady's having paid a compliment to a virtual stranger, Judith did not protest this high-handed arrangement of her time.

Furthermore, she was pleased to quit the drawing room, whatever the excuse. Hoping to escape before his lordship regained his tongue, she ushered the art lovers from the room, then through the hall and up the stone stairs to the next level, all with a most unseemly haste.

When they reached the gallery, which was at the front of the house, Judith was dismayed to find her sister there. Though Lilia had been reported as lying upon her bed, prostrate with the headache, she was, in fact, ensconced in her favorite chair, gazing dreamily out the window.

The chair, an over-sized, claw-footed monstrosity with a straight back and an uncushioned seat, appeared far too unyielding for relaxation; even so, the young girl had made herself comfortable. As if in defiance of the furniture's rigidity, she had abandoned her yellow kid slippers so that she might tuck her feet beneath her, the better to gaze out the window onto the park below.

"Lilia," Judith said in warning, "the visitors have arrived, and I have brought them for a tour of the gallery."

Startled, Miss Lilia Gillmore hurried to make herself presentable, slipping her dainty feet into the shoes, then standing and giving her sadly crushed sprigged muslin a quick shake. Blushing furiously, she reached her hand to the back of her head, where her coppery tresses had been drawn away from her face and fastened in a relaxed style. Reassured that no errant curls had bounced free of the coiffure, she bobbed a quick curtsy then clasped her hands before her, allowing her gaze to rest upon her interlaced fingers.

Actually, the young lady need not have been concerned for her appearance, for had she but known it, the gentlemen found nothing to dislike. To the contrary!

For his part, Andrew was spellbound. Though not much in the petticoat line, he stopped midway in the room, his usual polished manners deserting him, and stared at the vision as though she were one of the works of art on display.

Not that Zach faulted his brother for his lack of finesse. It would have been foolish to expect any other reaction, for Miss Lilia Gillmore was, without question, the prettiest girl Zachery Camden had ever seen.

With her dark brown eyes and her true English-rose complexion, not to mention a figure that was as near perfection as made no difference, she was the embodiment of every young man's dreams. Also, when she unbent so far as to favor Andrew with a shy smile—a not inconsiderable condescension, especially if she was being badgered by her grandfather into accepting the new heir as her husband-to-be—Zach mentally awarded her further points for good manners.

The young lady was reticent, and that reticence, coupled with her sister's objections—which had been stated earlier, and in no uncertain terms—were enough to convince Zach that they wanted no part of his lordship's scheme. Armed with the knowledge that he had only to guard against Lord Gillmore's machinations, Zach was able to relax his protective vigil for the moment.

Of course, the idea of a union between the distantly related pair was foolishness, plain and simple. Andrew had been in the military for less than a year, and because it was the career he had always dreamed of pursuing, taking a wife was the last thing on his mind. He was army mad and horse mad, and ladies followed quite some distance behind those other passions. As for Miss Lilia, she was still very young, probably no more than seventeen, and it was early days for her to be contemplating matrimony.

Furthermore, only an imbecile would think such a

beauty needed any help in snaring a husband. If Zach knew anything of human nature, every unattached male in the area—be he fifteen or fifty—would soon be paying the girl court.

"The picture you wished to see is this way," the wood nymph said, bringing Zach's thoughts back to the moment, "but first, allow me to make you known to my sister."

The introductions completed, Judith asked Lilia if she would show her cousin the half-dozen portraits of their jointly claimed ancestors, while she acquainted Mr. Camden with the Hogarth.

"Of course," Lilia said, keeping her eyes downcast. "This way, Lieutenant."

While the young couple strolled to the far end of the gallery, Zach turned his full attention upon Judith, as if taking her measure. "Do you think that was wise," he asked, "throwing them together? I thought you opposed the plan to unite them in wedlock."

"You were not mistaken, sir. I did, and I still do object to the scheme. Especially since I have never heard it reported that being forced into matrimony inspired affection in either of the parties."

"And that is your goal for your sister? Affection?"

"Yes. Affection and security, not to mention a husband she can respect. Not," she hurried to assure him, "that I find ought to dislike in your brother's character or manners."

"You relieve my mind," he said, his tone dry.

"Actually, Lieutenant Gillmore appears a most gentlemanlike person. It is only that I wish my sister to have the opportunity to follow the dictates of her heart."

While they strolled in the opposite direction from the portraits, Judith continued. "As for the wisdom of allowing my sister and your brother to view their ancestors in privacy, I see nothing to dislike in that. After all, you and I must be sufficient chaperones for a young couple in a single-room gallery, in broad daylight. Besides . . ."

"Besides?" he drawled, a hint of suspicion in the word.

Judith did not let his tone intimidate her, for she had something she wanted to ask of him—an idea whose possibilities she wished to explore. "There is something I would say to you in private."

"Somehow, madam, I thought there might be."

Wanting to give herself a few extra moments to frame her question, she said nothing more until they reached the Hogarth, which took pride of place, hanging in the middle of the wall at the top of the gallery.

"This canvas," Judith said, "is alleged to be one of a series of satirical paintings whose theme is marriage."

While they both regarded the painting, it was as if Judith saw it for the first time. No wonder her mother wanted Mr. Camden to see it!

Depicted in the foreground were three elderly, bewigged gentlemen who sat around a table, arguing the merits of a marriage contract. Meanwhile, sitting in a far corner, apparently bored by the entire procedure and each other, were the young lady and gentleman most particularly involved in the outcome.

After studying the painting for a few moments, Mr. Camden threw back his head and laughed, the deep sound echoing in the quiet room.

Though she admired his quickness in discerning her mother's message, she waited until his laughter died out before she spoke. "And do you?" she asked.

"Do I what?"

"Do you appreciate the painting's subtleties of line and color? My mother seemed to think you would, you being a *gentleman of discernment.*"

"A sentiment," he said, his dark brows lifted as if in acceptance of a challenge, "with which you do not agree."

"No, no. Acquit me, sir."

Judith pressed her lips together. She had already had one unfortunate interview with this man, and she could not afford to alienate him further. Not if she meant to ask for his assistance.

While leading the gentlemen from the drawing room, she had conceived of a foolproof plan—a plan that would insure Lilia's refusal to marry the heir. For her strategy to succeed, however, she needed a man of Zachery Camden's glib tongue and savoir faire. Never mind that he was the embodiment of everything she detested. If *she* could not say anything to influence her sister, lest she be the cause of having herself and her mother thrown from the premises without a penny to sustain them, then it behooved her to find someone *else* who could influence the girl.

"Actually," she said, "I am trying to find the proper words to put my luck, and your discernment, to the test."

His well-shaped lips curved slightly at the corners, in that slow, mocking smile she had noted earlier. "How very cryptic, ma'am. May one ask what you mean? Or is there another picture for me to examine?"

He stepped closer, as if to allow her to speak in confidence, and due to his height and the poke of her bonnet, Judith was obliged to tilt her head back to look up at him. It was a novel experience for a lady as tall as she, and one that caused an unexpected flutter in her midsection. "Sir, I . . . I wish to make you a wager."

For a moment, Zach thought he had not heard her correctly. "A wager?"

"Yes, sir. You are a gambler, are you not? A man who lives by his wits?"

"You could say that, I suppose. I have been known to take a chance from time to time."

Her wide, doe eyes looked up at him, the guileless blue orbs filled with uncertainty. "Will you take a chance with me?"

Zach gazed into her upturned, gamine's face, and knew a strong desire to be rid of her bonnet, to see that soft, ivory skin framed by her hair. Resisting the urge to reach up and loosen the ribbons himself, he said, "Forgive me, ma'am, but I make it a point never to make wagers with ladies."

The smile upon her lips was forced, as though his answer had been a setback, albeit one she did not wish to reveal. "Why the bias, sir? It was my understanding that a gentleman never refused a wager. To do so now, just because of my sex, is not at all sporting."

"Perhaps not, ma'am, but in my experience, it is the ladies who are not sporting. They seem never to have heard of Mr. Hoyle or of his book of rules."

Her smile faded. "But, sir, believe me, I would observe the principles of fair play."

Zach shook his head. "When ladies win, they are always quick to collect their prize, pocketing the money with the greatest joy. When they lose, however, the situation is quite different. Having lost, they will laugh and pretend the wager was all in jest, or they will resort to tears, insisting the fellow is a cad for taking their money when they had been saving it especially to purchase some *folderol* they felt certain he would like."

To his surprise, Miss Preston offered no rebuttal. Instead, she reached up and untied the ribbons of her straw bonnet. Then, as if she had somehow read his thoughts about wishing to see her hair, she removed the offending hat, revealing thick, shiny tresses of a soft medium brown.

Her coiffure was styled simply, being swept back from

her face and caught in a knot at the nape of her neck, and she had affected none of the busy curls worn by the fashionable ladies of London, choosing instead to allow her satiny forehead to remain as uncluttered as Heaven had designed it. As well, her cheeks were bare of sausage curls, leaving her pretty ears exposed to view.

While Zach looked his fill of the twin lobes, wondering if they felt as soft as they looked, the lady handed him the bonnet that still retained some of her warmth, then she reached inside the neck of her pelisse and withdrew a delicate gold chain. Suspended from the chain was an enameled heart, upon which was painted a single, gold-edged rose. Carefully she lifted the chain over her head. It was a snug fit, but she managed to remove it without mishap.

"Here," she said, offering the locket to him. "You may hold the stakes. If you should prove the winner, the necklace is yours. You have my promise that I will not renege, nor will I cry to have my property returned."

Zach glanced at the trinket before returning his attention to her serious countenance. It was obvious that her pride was at war with some other, stronger emotion, and he wondered as his gaze rested upon her soft, full lips, if she had any idea just how bewitching she was.

"Please," she said, "take it."

He did not do as she asked, but ran one of the bonnet ribbons through his fingers, listening to the soft *shush* of the satin. "You have not yet mentioned the sum you expect me to risk. Nor, if you recall, have you given voice to the actual wager."

The lady blushed. "What a ninnyhammer you must think me."

"No," he said slowly, setting the bonnet back upon her head, "I do not think you a ninnyhammer. If the truth be known, I have not yet decided what you are, though wisdom tells me that if I were prudent, I would remove myself from the range of those big blue eyes."

Judith could not think how she should reply to a remark that sounded suspiciously like flirtation, and before anything suggested itself to her, he reached out and began tying the ribbons beneath her chin, for all the world as though he had done it a million times before. The close contact had a disastrous effect upon the rhythm of her breathing, and as he gave the bow a final tug, his knuckles chanced to brush against that sensitive area just beneath her chin, leaving a trail of warmth upon her skin and causing her heart to miss a beat.

Very softly he asked, "Are you a sprite come to cast a spell upon me? Or merely an elf come to throw magic dust in my eyes?"

Sprite? Elf? Were those gaming terms? If so, Judith had never heard them before. In any case, she shook her head. "I am merely a lady who wishes to do all within her power to insure the happiness of a beloved sister."

He searched her face for a moment; then, obviously satisfied with what he found there, he took the locket from her hand and slipped it into the fob pocket of his dove-gray brocade waistcoat. "I shall hazard a golden guinea," he said. "Fair enough?"

She breathed a sigh of relief. "Quite."

"So," he said, "the stakes are agreed upon. It remains only for us to discuss the nature of the contest."

Judith cleared her throat, nervous now that he had all but agreed to her plan. "It is very simple, sir. I wager my locket against your golden guinea that you cannot make my sister fall in love with you."

Three

"Madam, you must think me a fool!"

"N-no, sir. I—"

"If not a fool, then an unconscionable libertine."

Zach could tell from the way she suddenly lowered her eyelids, as if to keep him from reading the truth in her eyes, that a libertine was exactly what she thought him. How she had come to such a conclusion, he could not imagine, but if that was her opinion, what had possessed her to suggest he play fast and loose with her sister's heart?

Had she somehow discovered that he was a man of considerable wealth, and that his brother had no money save his soldier's pay and the occasional gifts the lad accepted from him? Was that it? She had told Zach earlier that she wanted security for her sister. Was she seeking the larger purse, and hoping to compromise him into offering for the girl?

"I would like to know, madam, upon what basis you formed your opinion that I am the kind of loose screw who would trifle with the affections of a young lady of such tender years?"

She looked up at him, and there was such pleading in her eyes that he relented somewhat.

"Have you a distrust of all men," he asked, "or only me?"

Somehow, Judith found her voice. "Truly, sir, I meant no insult. In my desire to have all settled, I did not state my wishes as clearly as I should have liked. I do not desire that you break Lilia's heart, merely engage her interest to such an extent that she would think herself in a fair way to forming a *tendre*."

"In other words," he said, "you expect me to trifle with her affections."

"Not at all. I just . . ."

She sighed, not knowing how to continue. She had insulted him. Yet, who would have thought a gambler would take such offense? *She* had certainly not expected it. Especially since she had been led to believe that sporting men would accept any wager, no matter how base.

Had she not heard with her own ears some of the more famous, albeit mindless, contests upon which large sums of money had changed hands? Had her own father not risked all upon a foolish whim?

Though her mother had tried to keep from Judith the story of George Preston's lifestyle, she had overheard a version of the story when she was scarcely more than nine or ten years old. She and her mother had gone to the draper's for a length of blue merino suitable for a warm school dress, and while in the store, Judith wandered over to the notions stacks to admire the myriad of ribbons, laces, and buttons. It was while she bent down to look at a roll of bobbin lace stored on one of the lower shelves that she overheard two village women gossiping about her father. George Preston had been dead a half dozen years at this time, but his suicide was still prominent on the villagers' list of exciting topics.

"Killed 'imself, did 'er first 'usband," the woman said, fingering a bolt of cheap muslin as if to persuade any onlookers that she was contemplating a purchase. "The way my Jem tells it, Mr. Preston bet another gentleman five thousand quid 'e could catch a fly in one 'and."

"Never say so!" replied her listener. "Five thousand pounds on a fly?"

"Lost it all, of course. After three tries, when 'e 'ad failed to catch the insect, 'e went double or nothing for another go at it. Lost that time too."

Her listener made a *tsk-tsk* noise with her tongue. "What happened then?"

"Next day 'e shot 'imself."

As if that story were not enough to make Judith turn her face against all gamblers, several years later, when she was in London for her come-out, she heard similar tales of enormous wagers placed upon the result of such foolishness as the capture of greased pigs, or the exact number of stripes in a certain gentleman's waistcoat. As for cock-fighting and bear-baiting, she did not even want to think of those despicable pursuits, or the men who risked their fortunes and the welfare of their families upon the outcomes.

With such tales in her memory, how could she have expected Zachery Camden to cavil at charming a young girl into believing herself in love with him. While she tried to think of a way to make him understand, she heard the echo of footfalls and knew the lieutenant and her sister were approaching.

"I cannot explain myself now, sir. Would you meet me in the west garden in an hour?"

When he hesitated, she felt herself blushing. "You need not be afraid of meeting me privately, for I do not wish you to make *me* fall in love with you. Not that you could, of course."

Judith wondered what she had said to make that devilish spark appear in his eyes, but before she could ask, the spark had vanished, almost as if it had been a figment of her imagination. "Will you do it?" she asked.

"Madam, I am tempted."

The devilish spark might have been an illusion, but Judith was quite certain she did not imagine that movement at the corners of his mouth! The man was trying not to laugh!

"Yes," he said, "I am sorely tempted."

"What think you of him?" Judith asked.

Her mother closed the cap on the inkpot and laid the quill in the curled lip of the brass stand. After dusting the single sheet of paper with pounce to keep the ink from running, she set the unfinished letter inside the rosewood writing box that was the last present Albert Gillmore had given her before his death. "He seems a gentlemanly sort of young man, and not at all what I had expected. I believe I like him. But what of you? Did you form an opinion of Lieutenant Gillmore?"

Lieutenant Gillmore?

Judith only just that minute realized that she had given little thought to the future heir. She had, in fact, spent much of the last half hour since parting from the gentleman trying to decipher the enigma that was the lieutenant's older brother. Playing for time, she sauntered over to the other side of her mother's bedchamber and placed her pelisse and bonnet upon the small green velvet stool at the foot of the domed bed. Once there, she lifted a corner of the cream and green hangings, pushing her finger through a rent.

"Another mending job, Mother."

Mrs. Gillmore sighed. "I have mended those hangings so often this past year that I should not be at all surprised to discover that my stitches comprise nine-tenths of the material."

Her mother's bedchamber, a once-handsome room used in former times for honored guests, was directly opposite the gallery, and Judith had chosen to visit there because she did not wish to join Lilia in the bedchamber and dressing room they shared. Worried that she might say something his lordship could use against her, Judith preferred to delay any private time spent with her sister until after she had met with Mr. Camden.

"The lieutenant is young," Judith said finally.

"True," her mother replied. "Not quite two and twenty. Do you think that circumstance an asset or a liability?"

"I have no way of knowing. One often hears it said that very young brides make fewer mistakes with an older, more experienced husband to guide them. Yet I cannot help but wonder if extreme disparity in the couple's ages does not contribute to boredom much earlier in the marriage than might be expected. After all, what can two people with such different experiences have to say to one another?"

"Then you think it is a point in the gentleman's favor that he is close to Lilia's own age?"

"How can I say, when we know nothing of the lieutenant's financial situation? As a rule, young gentlemen must look to their parents for some sort of allowance. This is so even if they have chosen one of the professions, and while—"

"Judith, my love. I was speaking of the possibility of their forming a *tendre* for one another. You speak only of finances."

"I speak of security, Mama. A woman dare not let her heart rule her head. Otherwise, she may well find herself a widow with no money and no home to call her own."

"Like me," Dorothy Gillmore said softly.

She went to her mother, taking the lady's hands in her own. "Exactly like you. Forgive me, Mama, if the subject causes you pain, but you must see that if Lilia marries Lord Gillmore's heir, and he has no income other than his army pay, then her situation will be identical to yours when you married Papa Albert. She and her husband will be dependent upon his lordship for every penny."

She searched her mother's face. "Having lived through that yourself, is that what you wish for your daughter?"

Mrs. Gillmore shook her head. "I do not wish it. But what alternative do we have?"

Judith shrugged her shoulders. "None, I suppose."

As if wishing to weigh all sides, her mother said, "Theirs would not be an unsuitable match, you know, and there is one definite advantage."

"And that is?"

"Since it is within the family, so to speak, the absence of a bride's portion might be overlooked. As you well know, your sister has no dowry to bring to a marriage."

Judith sighed. "Still, I cannot help but believe that with Lilia's beauty, a lack of dowry may not matter so greatly. If only she is not rushed into an early commitment, other opportunities may present themselves."

"We have resided in Blinbourne for almost a year."

"Yes, but during most of that period we were in mourning for Papa Albert. For all we know, there may be some perfectly respectable gentleman who has seen Lilia at church, or in the village, and is already enamored of her. Some gentleman who has been waiting for the proper moment to make his feelings known, waiting only until you put off your black to broach the matter. We need time to—"

"Time," Mrs. Gillmore said, "is such an unreliable element. When we want it to hurry, it refuses to do so, and yet it seems always to fly when we most want it to stand still."

"And," Judith added, "should time be so obliging as to remain in place, a person may depend upon it that her finances will turn perverse and flee as if possessed of winged feet."

"No truer words were ever spoken, my love. Finances must always be coaxed to linger. Even when I practice the most stringent economy, the twenty-five pounds per annum left me by my Aunt Elsbeth never lasts a full twelvemonth. In fact, the money is usually a memory long before Michaelmas. Which is, of course, why I had hoped to remain at Gillmore House until both you and Lilia found suitable husbands.

"Once the two of you were settled," she continued, "it was my ambition to rent a small cottage situated near one of you. In a simpler environment, I had hoped the twenty-five pounds would serve, allowing me to live if not grandly, at least independently."

Judith kept to herself her suspicion that she and her mother might both be forced to occupy that small cottage and live upon Aunt Elsbeth's twenty-five pounds per annum. Dorothy Gillmore might still believe that both her daughters would wed, but Judith cherished no such expectations. No longer in her first blush of youth, and without a dowry, her chances for contracting a suitable alliance were practically nonexistent. Actually, the likelihood of her forming a less-than-suitable alliance was not all that strong.

Not that the thought of such a union inspired Judith with any great degree of pleasure. Though she might expound upon the importance of financial security in marriage, deep within her was a desire to know how it felt to love a man with all her heart and be loved by him in return. In the depths of her soul, she longed to experience the joy and ecstasy of being in the arms of a man she adored. To share his kisses. To feel his heart beating in unison with her own.

Hearts beating as one? Bah! Mere rhetoric. A hoax played upon unwitting females to insure the continuation of the human race.

Calling herself a fool for cleaving to such adolescent fantasy, Judith weighed her hypothetical options. Love or security? Passion or porridge? A realist, she did not expect the two to go hand in hand. And yet, it frightened her to think she might one day surrender her dream of love, might marry for the sake of a roof over her head.

Realizing that her mother had continued to talk, Judith called herself to attention. After all, it was not *her* future that was of importance at the moment, it was Lilia's. Lieutenant Gillmore and his brother would be here for a fortnight, and within those two weeks, Lord Gillmore expected to bring about an engagement.

It was Judith's job to see he failed.

Unfortunately, she had come up with only one plan to thwart his lordship, and that was to have Lilia refuse to marry the heir because she loved another. Of course, convincing that *other* to make Lilia fall in love with him had not proven as easy as she had hoped.

Judith recalled the way the gambler had looked at her while his long, tapered fingers tied her bonnet strings beneath her chin. She had stood unmoving, very nearly mesmerized by his eyes. Honesty compelled her to admit that even though her task of convincing him to accept the wager was proving difficult, his task, once he accepted it, should prove an easy assignment.

Why should it not? It must be obvious to even the most unromantic female that Zachery Camden was the type of man any girl would find appealing. Tall, handsome, and possessing a decidedly masculine physique, there was also about him a roguish, almost dangerous quality that was strangely attractive.

An inexperienced girl like Lilia would be putty in his hands!

Realizing that the allotted hour had very nearly passed, and that Mr. Camden might even now be waiting for her in the garden, Judith excused herself to her mother and all but ran down the stone steps, lifting the hem of her muslin frock so she did not trip. Avoiding the front entrance, she employed her usual route, which led her through the door that gave off the rear of the hall and down a long corridor past the housekeeper's room and the kitchen.

Once outside, she followed a flagstone path to a small rustic garden where a dozen pear trees were in full bloom, their delicate white blossoms a perfect companion to the pink and lavender thrift that blanketed the surrounding area. In the midst of the small garden were two wrought-iron benches, and it was toward those benches that Judith hurried.

Zach spotted her before she saw him. Not in the garden itself, he stood some way off, on a gently rising knoll, leaning against a very old, very tall Scotch pine. He had been there for some time, enjoying the fragrant spring air and listening to the low, rather melancholy *chat chat chat* of a distant stonechat as the black-capped bird flitted restlessly from the top of one gorse bush to another.

Zach did not call out a greeting, but allowed himself a few moments to watch Judith Preston as she traversed the path on her way to the garden. She had discarded her bonnet and pelisse and wore a simple muslin frock whose pale green was the shade of newly unfurled leaves. Circling the frock's high waist was a moss green ribbon, and the colors seemed to strengthen Zach's fancy that she was a creature of the forest.

Her figure in no way resembled Miss Lilia's perfect proportions, yet there was a gracefulness to her slender shape that Zach found particularly appealing. It was odd, when he recalled the voluptuous ladybirds who had enjoyed his protection over the past few years, that her modest bosom should so attract his interest.

She had arrived at a small bench, and was about to dispose herself upon it when she suddenly turned. Obviously she had felt him watching her, for she looked directly at him. For a moment, neither of them moved, almost as though needing to re-evaluate one another in this newer, more natural environment. When he would have joined her in the garden, she waved him back and met him instead upon the grassy knoll.

"If you should not dislike it," she said by way of greeting, "I would like to walk a bit."

"My pleasure," he replied. "But you must promise to let me know when you begin to tire."

"That would be never."

"Never?" He gave her a mocking look. "Such a passionate reply makes me wonder, Miss Preston, if you are a dedicated nature lover, a proponent of fresh air and exercise, or merely a young woman given to exaggeration."

Judith could not stop the smile that sprang to her lips. "Exaggeration? Me? Not in a million years."

Only his gray eyes smiled. "Minx!" he said, as he caught her hand and placed it in the crook of his arm. "Come, Wood Nymph, and show me your real home."

She withdrew her hand. "What did you call me?"

"A minx. Surely you have heard the term before. It means a pert—"

"Not that. The other."

He caught her hand again, and this time, when he placed it in the crook of his arm, he did not let go of her fingertips.

"Do you mean to make me repeat everything I say, or shall we take that walk?"

When he took the first step, she followed suit, and to Zach's surprise and pleasure, she did not mince in the fashion of London ladies out for an afternoon stroll to exhibit themselves and their finery. To the contrary. She walked briskly, purposefully, and as they progressed down one gentle green slope and up the next, he never once had to slow his pace to allow her to keep up.

For a number of minutes they said nothing, both content to regard the blue, cloudless sky, the rolling green combes and vales that could be seen for miles ahead, and the flocks of Dorset sheep, with their distinctive curled horns and their fleece as fine and white as freshly fallen snow.

"I have missed this," she said, breaking the comfortable silence. "Before we came to Blinbourne, I used to lead a very active life—a ride every morning, long rambles in the woods, and almost daily walks with my sister to the village."

"It sounds quite invigorating."

"It was. And I cannot tell you how much I loved it. Especially the occasional excursions we made to the cliffs to sketch the channel as it crashed against the shore. It was magnificent there, for the force of the waves constantly cut away at the soft clay, while leaving the stronger stones intact, thereby guaranteeing that the scenery was never the same from one visit to the next."

Noting the enthusiasm with which she talked, and the liveliness of her facial expression, Zach wished he might have been with her on those excursions to the chalk cliffs. "You said you *used* to lead an active life. I know you have been in mourning, but I cannot believe even the strictest

of parents would find anything to censure in such innocent
pastimes."

"The impediment lies not with my mother, but with Lord
Gillmore. He professes to dislike the notion of females
racketing about the countryside."

"You said, 'professes.' An odd choice of words. Do you
not take him at his word?"

She shook her head. "I believe his dislike has a great
deal more to do with parsimony than with propriety. If we
had horses, he would be obliged to stable and feed them."

"Ah, yes. I see your point."

They said nothing for some time more, then Zach asked
her if there were riding horses to be hired in the village.

"There are, sir, but if you and Lieutenant Gillmore wish
to see some of the countryside, I believe you would do
better to present yourselves to his lordship's neighbor, Sir
Thomas Rainsford. Sir Thomas has some of the finest
horses in the area."

"Raises them himself, does he?"

"Actually, it is his son, Mr. Stanbury Rainsford, who is
most nearly involved with the animals. Though Stanbury
is not yet twenty-one, he has a knowledge of horseflesh
beyond his years."

The discussion of horses was cut short when she pointed
toward a weir perhaps a quarter of a mile away. "That is
our destination," she said, freeing her arm from his and
breaking into a run.

Once Zach had recovered from the shock of a young
lady lifting her skirts and sprinting away, her athletic ability
evident in the speed with which she was covering the distance to the brook, he began to run also. Quite fit himself,
he was able to catch up with her, though he was careful
not to pass her by and spur her to a speed that might prove
injurious to her well-being.

He need not have worried, however, for when they reached the weir, her breathing was only slightly ragged, and her face glowed with healthy color.

His senses already heightened by the unexpected race, Zach found himself inordinately interested in the rise and fall of her small bosom as her breathing resumed its normal pace.

"Here we are," she said, bestowing upon him a lovely, unpretentious smile that revealed straight, even teeth. "What do you think?

"I think," he said, his gaze fastened upon her soft, beguiling mouth, "that I would like very much to—"

Zach stopped himself in time, only just realizing that his face was mere inches from hers, and that he had been about to kiss her. Not that he was as surprised by the idea as he might have been, considering their exhilarating romp across the land and that beautiful smile, but he felt quite certain the wood nymph would be astonished at such presumption.

"I would like to know," he said, as though in continuation of his original thought, "why you brought me here."

The weir, when he took time to notice it, was nothing more than an unimaginative wooden structure erected across a small stream. Its sole purpose was to dam the waters, thereby raising them to a level suitable for fishing. Unimpressed with the sight after the lovely pastoral scenery they had enjoyed for the last hour, Zach asked if this spot held some special significance for her.

"It was but a goal," she replied. "And though I should like to keep walking until I reached the cliffs, I know that is not feasible."

"And do you always have a goal?"

"Whenever possible, I prefer to know where I am going. Life has visited a number of surprises upon me lately—things over which I have no control—and for that reason, I like to take charge of those few things still within my power. Unlike you," she added, "I do not like to gamble."

The moment the words left her mouth, Judith had the grace to blush, for she remembered that he still retained her locket, the evidence that she had become that very thing she abhorred, a gambler. In fact, their unresolved wager was her purpose for being in his company. How could she have forgotten?

Not wanting him to witness her confusion, she turned and began to retrace her steps, never once looking back to see if he followed. When he finally joined her, she seized the chance to explain to him why she wanted him to make Lilia fall in love with him.

"Lord Gillmore," she began, "is a man accustomed to having his orders obeyed, and before this day is done, I expect he will order your brother to marry my sister. The lieutenant may refuse, of course, but that will not stop his lordship. If nothing else works, he is not above claiming that Lilia has been compromised in some way, thereby forcing your brother to do the honorable thing."

"And what of Miss Lilia? Has she no say in the matter?"

"Lilia is still very young. She is accustomed to having others make decisions for her, and I fear that unless she has a reason to rebel, she will allow herself to be coerced into doing as her grandfather orders."

"You are her sister, why do you not simply tell her what you think is best for her to do?

"I cannot. Lord Gillmore has forbidden it, under penalty of . . ." Judith pressed her lips together, not wanting to reveal the embarrassing state of her family's finances, or the fact that they were living on Lord Gillmore's charity.

"Somehow," Zach said, "I had not thought you were afraid of his lordship."

"I am not."

"Then can you not tell me the whole?" he asked softly.

When she continued to walk, he put his hand beneath her elbow and stopped her, turning her so that she was obliged to look up at him. "Do not be embarrassed. Believe me, you are not the first person to reside with someone who merely tolerates you."

"You?"

He circumvented her question, choosing to say instead, "I suspect, Miss Preston, that we have much in common."

He offered no further explanation, and that mask he used with such efficacy descended once again. Curiously, it was that reticence to expose his own experience that convinced Judith that he did, indeed, understand her plight.

"I want to protect my sister, but Lord Gillmore has made it perfectly clear that if I interfere with his plans, my mother and I will no longer be welcome at Gillmore House. Not that I wish to remain under his roof, you understand. I would leave gladly if we had any other place to go. Unfortunately, because Papa Albert, my stepfather, had no income of his own—only that allowance made him by his lordship—my mother was not provided for."

"So," Zach said softly, "faced with a seemingly hopeless situation, you have resorted to making wagers with strangers."

Judith nodded, happy he had grasped the situation so quickly.

With everything now out in the open, and nothing more to be said, they fell into step again, briskly covering the rolling green landscape, the only sound an occasional bleat from sheep startled by the sudden appearance of two unknown humans.

They were within sight of the garden and the white-blossomed pear trees before their silence was broken. "Very well," Zach said. "How much in love with me do you wish Miss Lilia to be?"

Four

Judith was unprepared for the sick feeling that invaded the pit of her stomach. Zachery Camden had agreed to set up a flirtation with Lilia, and Judith should have been rejoicing. Instead, she felt unaccountably sad.

No, not sad. Jealous!

Foolish beyond permission, of course. What right had she to be jealous of her own sister. Her innocent sister! Lilia had scarce said two words to the man. As for Mr. Camden, a person Judith had met little more than four hours ago, he might set up a flirtation with a hundred chits—nay, a thousand—and it would be no concern of hers.

He meant nothing to her, nor she to him. Admittedly, she had enjoyed being in his company. What woman would not? Conversing with him was easy; even *not* conversing with him was easy.

In the past, Judith had been uncomfortable in the presence of handsome, assured gentlemen; however, with Zachery Camden she had exhibited none of her usual reserve. With him she had been herself, unhampered by the necessity to adhere to society's accepted behavior. There was no deferring to his wishes or his moods simply because he was the male and she the female, and by the time they had reached the weir, Judith felt almost as if they were friends.

Of course, he might not have felt as she did. Possibly that feeling of camaraderie existed only in her imagination. She had certainly imagined one or two other things.

Like that kiss!

Not that there had actually been a kiss. It was just some fancy that had taken hold of her thoughts. When they first reached the weir, she had conceived of a quite ridiculous notion that he wanted to kiss her.

Because she had run the last quarter mile, her breathing was uneven, and she could feel her heart beating rapidly inside her chest. To her dismay, when she turned and looked up at him, her heart went from a rapid beat to a thunderous pounding, for his gaze was fixed upon her mouth, and there was in his eyes an undeniable warmth. Though Judith had never seen that look before, she thought she understood it.

When he took a step toward her, then leaned down, his face very close to hers, some instinct—some womanly knowledge as old as time—told her she was about to be kissed.

Womanly knowledge, indeed!

She had very nearly made a fool of herself. While her heart pounded like the hooves of a hundred galloping horses, she had waited shamelessly for Zachery Camden to lean down those final few inches. In another second she would have been offering him her lips. Thankfully, he chose that moment to turn and look at the weir, thereby saving her and himself from certain embarrassment.

"Since we are agreed upon the wager," he said, breaking in upon her thoughts, "it wants only for us to seal the bargain with a handshake."

"Mr. Camden, I—"

"Please, if we are to be coconspirators against Lord Gillmore, I should like it if you would call me Zach."

He continued to hold his hand out to her, and good manners dictated that she acknowledge the gesture. When Judith placed her hand in his, he did not shake it as she had expected, but lifted it to his lips, placing a warm kiss upon her knuckles. At the touch of his mouth upon her skin, a current of sensation sped from her fingers directly to her lungs, colliding with that organ so forcefully that she was robbed of the breath needed to say his name.

Unable to speak, and unwilling to reveal to him the effect of that simple kiss upon her senses, Judith slipped her hand from his, bobbed a quick curtsy, and fled past the garden and up to the house.

"If I remember correctly," Andrew said, answering his hostess's question regarding the newest member of the royal family, "they christened her Alexandrina Victoria."

"How beautiful," Mrs. Gillmore replied, smiling at the lieutenant, who occupied the place directly to her right at the ornate walnut dining table. "So very regal sounding. If she should one day ascend to the throne, it would be a fitting name for a queen."

After serving himself a portion of baked carp that had been dressed in the Portuguese way, Andrew returned the serving spoons to the tray held by the footman, then he gave his attention back to the discussion. "According to the account in yesterday's *Times,* ma'am, the full name was not settled upon until mere seconds before the archbishop christened the newborn."

"Why ever not?" Miss Preston asked.

He looked at the young lady who sat across the table from him. Dressed in rose-colored sarcenet, she appeared rather pretty, though nothing to compare with Miss Lilia, whose reddish brown curls were laced through with a silver ribbon in a manner that was as charming as it was artless.

"It seems that Prinny favored the name Georgina, ma'am, while the Duke and Duchess of Kent preferred Victoria."

The topic obviously exhausted, Andrew took the opportunity to sample one or two of the dishes before him. The food and wine were quite good, and considering the unpleasantness that had erupted the last time they were all congregated, the evening meal was progressing pleasantly. If the conversation was not scintillating, at least it was civil, with Mrs. Gillmore and Miss Preston informing him of those sights they had most enjoyed when they were in town some years ago, and him supplying such *on dits* about the royal family as he thought they might find interesting.

Unfortunately, Lord Gillmore chose that moment to contribute his mite to the discussion.

"We need a king!" he said, punctuating the remark with a sharp whack of his cane against the table leg. "I do not hold with the notion of female heirs."

Into the silence that followed this unanswerable bias, Zach advised his lordship not to despair. "If the gossips are to be believed, the Duke of Clarence and his new lady have not conceded the race to produce the next sovereign. There may yet be a male heir. Of a certainty, the betting books at the clubs are filled with wagers made upon that likelihood."

"Speaking of races," Andrew said, hoping to introduce a subject less likely to raise the ire of the old martinet, "I heard something only this morning about a horse race to be run in this area. I collect the time was within the next week, but I am not certain of the exact day. Can you tell me anything of it, sir?"

Although Miss Lilia had not looked up from her plate nor spoken since the meal began, at the mention of the race she jumped, knocking over her water glass. After muttering some sort of apology, she snatched her napkin from her lap and began to mop at the liquid that threatened to spill over the edge of the table.

"Damnation!" Lord Gillmore said, glaring at Andrew. "Never tell me you are one of those young care-for-nobodies who waste the ready on riotous living."

"No, no," Andrew corrected. "You quite misunderstand the matter, sir. 'Tis the horses I love."

"Be warned," his lordship said, pointing his cane at him as though he were a recalcitrant schoolboy. "If you've a penchant for gaming, you need not think you can come to me to pull you out of the River Tick. I'll not do it, and you had best understand that fact from the start."

His good nature breached at last, Andrew said, "Rest assured, sir, that if I should find myself in difficulty for any reason, I know to whom I may apply." He looked toward Zach. "I have always known it. As for chancing my luck with money, I leave such matters to my brother, for he has a quite uncanny knack with—"

"I do not care what your brother does!" his lordship shouted. "It is no concern of mine if the fellow goes from one gaming hell to another, risking whatever money he may have. Let him end his days in a sponging house if that is his wish. What I want you to understand, Gillmore, is that—"

"Sponging house!" Andrew rose from the table, tossing his napkin aside. "Sir! Allow me to inform you that my brother is—"

"Quite able to speak for himself," Zach finished for him. "Now sit down, Andrew, there's a good fellow. I dare say Mrs. Gillmore is heartily sick of such poor dinner conversation and is wishing the lot of us to the antipodes."

Bringing his temper under control, Andrew bowed first to Dorothy Gillmore and then to both her daughters. "Beg pardon, ma'am, Miss Preston, Cousin Lilia, for my want of manners."

"That is quite all right," Judith said, passing her napkin across the table to her sister, who was still mopping up the water she had spilled. "We think nothing of bad manners here. Believe me, they are our daily fare."

It was mid-morning before Judith saw either of the gentlemen again. By common consent, the ladies had left the table last evening following the contretemps between Lord Gillmore and his heir, taking themselves off to their respective bedchambers without going to the drawing room to await the arrival of the tea tray. As for the gentlemen, Peasby had informed Judith the next morning that while his lordship had occupied his usual place beside the drawing room fire, the future heir and Mr. Camden had spent the remainder of the evening in the billiard room.

"And a rare taking his lordship was in, miss," the butler added. "Threw his cane at poor Charles's head when the fellow informed him that the lieutenant declined his offer to join him for a brandy."

Though Judith expressed her sympathy for the poor footman, and hoped he had not sustained any serious injury, she was pleased with the information that no tête-à-tête had taken place between Lord Gillmore and his heir. If there had been no private talk, that meant the lieutenant's hand had not yet been forced, for even the devil himself would have better manners than to inform a young man of his coming betrothal while a third party was within earshot.

"Where are the visitors now?" she asked.

"Gone out this hour and more, miss. John Coachman drove them over to Rainsford Manor so they might speak with Sir Thomas regarding the acquisition of saddle horses for the fortnight. It seems Mr. Camden has a desire to see the cliffs."

Judith was not the only person who was happy the subject of marriage had not been broached last evening. Zach was quite relieved. Each day they avoided that particular conversation was one day closer to their scheduled departure and a safe escape. If he could keep his brother in company at all times, thereby putting a period to any chance Lord Gillmore might have for that private talk, perhaps the old gentleman would give over this foolish scheme to promote a match between his granddaughter and his heir.

As for Zach's trying his hand at winning Miss Lilia's affections, he would leave that strategy until such time as it became absolutely necessary. For the moment, he contented himself with finding ways to insure that the young lady and his brother were never left without a chaperone of some kind. With that purpose in mind, he had suggested driving over to Rainsford Manor to inquire about leasing horses.

Within little more than a quarter hour, the coachman halted the chaise before the portico of the new, and unconscionably ornate brick mansion belonging to Sir Thomas Rainsford. While Andrew stared open-mouthed at the profusion of gargoyles decorating the chimney tops and the corners of the house, Zach stepped down to the gravel carriageway, contenting himself with reading the motto carved above the heavy oak entrance doors.

"My word," Andrew said, almost falling over his brother, "what does it say? 'In for a pence, in for a pound?' "

"Mind your tongue," Zach warned, then he read the words aloud. *"Humani nil a me alienum puto."*

With an unselfconscious shrug, Andrew said, "I fear my Latin is a bit rusty."

"Mine as well, but as near as I can translate, it says, 'Nothing that concerns man is foreign to my interests.' "

"Right you are, sir," said the middle-aged man who swung open the oak doors.

Expecting to see a butler, Zach was momentarily taken aback to discover a man dressed in a florid yellow waistcoat worn beneath a puce satin coat. A short, thick-set fellow, he was obliged to hold his head still, moving it to neither left nor right, owing to the extreme height and stiffness of his starched shirt points.

"Come in. Come in," invited the gentleman, who could only be the master of the house. His flyaway hair, a mixture of gray and sandy blond, did nothing to tone down his ruddy complexion, and it was that permanently sunburned skin that betrayed him for what he was—or what he used to be—a yeoman farmer. In view of the ostentatious display of new house and clothes, it was obvious the farmer—knighted for some reason or other—aspired to moving beyond the station of his birth.

"Good morning," Zach said, executing a bow formal enough to satisfy even the most discriminating stickler. "Pray forgive us for calling upon you unannounced, Sir Thomas, and allow me to introduce myself. I am—"

"No need for that, sir. Knew who you were the minute I saw Lord Gillmore's coachman up on the box of this bang-up chaise." He eyed the gold-trimmed maroon traveling coach with apparent pleasure. "His lordship don't own an equipage anywhere near as fine as this. Not by a longshot he don't."

Zach inclined his head politely. "I am pleased you like—"

" 'Course, his lordship being the eighth baron and all, he can ride around in that old moth-eaten coach of his and people don't give it a thought. You and me, now, we like something a bit more modern, don't we, sir?"

Having been neatly relegated to the ranks of the *nouveau riche*. Zach thought it prudent to give Andrew's arm a warning squeeze, just in case that loyal relative felt obliged once again to defend his brother's honor.

"Since you were so quick to deduce who we are," Zach said pleasantly, "I will be disappointed if you cannot guess, as well, why we have called. Should you need a hint, allow me to inform you that the word is your horses have no equal in the neighborhood."

Sir Thomas's red face beamed. "Nor in the entire shire, sir, though I say it as shouldn't. But come," he said, motioning toward a pair of neat brick stables that could be seen at some distance to the left, "a picture is worth a thousand words, don't you know."

No matter what anyone might think of Sir Thomas Rainsford and his almost comical bid to be accepted as a gentleman, not even his biggest detractors could doubt his having been a savvy and hardworking farmer, not if his stables were anything to judge by.

The twenty-stalls within the first stable, each one a neat ten feet by ten feet, were the most modern and efficient Zach had ever seen, their wooden floors cleaner than many a gentleman's house, with the sweet-smelling straw freshly laid that morning. There were four grooms busy watering the horses, and though they pulled their forelocks in greeting to the master and his visitors, each went immediately back to his duties.

"These," Sir Thomas said proudly, "are the racing horses. I know you gentlemen came to see riding cattle, but being as you are here, I thought you might like a quick look."

"Rather!" Andrew agreed, looking around him with renewed interest. "Are any of these horses racing next week?"

"At Abbotsbury, do you mean?"

"I suppose that is the location. I overheard some fellows talking at an inn in Dorcester, and I wondered where the meet would be held."

"Abbotsbury," Sir Thomas repeated. "But to answer your question, I'll not be taking any of my animals there. For one thing, it is a *heat,* and I don't hold with such, they're too hard on the horses. A four-mile run, with the horses pitted head to head? No sir! Not from this stable. For another thing," he added, "the meet is for three-year-old fillies, and we have only one such here, Stanbury's Bess. And she belongs to my son."

"If it would not be too much trouble," Andrew said, "may we see her?"

"Certainly, Lieutenant. She's in stall number seven, across from that bay stallion who is showing his oats."

The spirited stallion, a handsome, straight-backed Arabian, snorted and pawed the ground as Andrew and Zach walked past, so they did not stop. Instead, they went directly to the filly's stall. Attached above the stall was a brass nameplate, upon which was etched the number seven and Stanbury's Bess. Not wanting to startle the animal, the gentlemen paused a moment to speak to the young groom who held an oak pail from which the roan was daintily sipping water.

"May we approach?" Zach asked.

"You may, sir," he replied in a cultured voice. "Bess is not easily spooked.

Expecting something quite different, Zach looked more

closely at the slender young man with the sunny blond hair. Though he was dressed in corduroy breeches and a work-man's smock, much as the other lads in the stable, from the assurance with which he spoke, it was apparent that he was no groom. That fact was confirmed a moment later when Sir Thomas caught up with them.

"I see you have met my son," he said. "Stanbury, my boy, make your bow to Mr. Camden and Lieutenant Gill-more."

A handsome young man of perhaps twenty years of age, he nodded politely at Zach. "Sir," he said. When he looked at Andrew, however, the nod was not quite so polite, and his brown eyes were distinctly cold.

"Have we met before?" Andrew asked. Then before the young man had a chance to answer, he said, "Stanbury Rainsford? The name has a familiar ring to it."

Sir Thomas beamed as though someone had handed him first prize at a race. "Were you at Harrow, Lieutenant? My boy was there."

Andrew snapped his fingers, happy to have a riddle solved. "That is it. You were the next form down from me."

Though young Rainsford mumbled something that passed for a civil reply, his manner was still decidedly cool, and Zach wondered what could account for it. Surely he was not still holding some schoolboy grudge.

"Well, now," Sir Thomas said, "if that don't show what a small world it is. When Miss Lilia was here the other day, telling us that his lordship's heir was due to arrive in a few days, I never dreamed he would turn out to be one of Stan's old school chums."

He laughed suddenly, as though remembering a good jest. "I'll tell you to your face, Gillmore, that when the chit told us you were in the army, I warned her to put her heart in a safe place and lock it up tight while you were here.

Made her blush pretty as a bush full of roses, but it was good advice, for I never saw a female yet who didn't make a spectacle of herself over a red coat. Even my missus, God rest her soul, had always a soft spot for a fellow in uniform."

He winked at Andrew. "Careful how you go, lad, or you'll be turning Miss Lilia's pretty head."

While Andrew made a perfunctory attempt at a polite reply, Zach gave his attention to Mr. Stanbury Rainsford, for upon hearing his father relate the advice he had given Miss Lilia regarding the safekeeping of her heart, that young man had stiffened noticeably. As for the conjecture that she might find a uniform to her liking, that cheerfully stated possibility had the lad fairly grinding his teeth.

So, that is the way the wind blows.

At least it appeared to blow that way where young Mr. Rainsford was concerned. Not that it was to be marveled at if two handsome young people, their homes scare a mile apart, should seek each other out. What could be more logical?

But what of Miss Lilia?

Recalling that the young lady had knocked over her water glass last evening when Andrew mentioned the race, Zach suspected she might cherish at least a degree of interest in those matters pertaining to the young race horse owner. Of course, if she did, her sister was not privy to the information, else Judith would not be seeking someone to make the girl think she was in love.

An interesting turn of events, Zach decided, and one that bore looking into.

Five

Though it was not one of her usual reading places, Judith chanced to be seated on one of the rosewood settees in the hall, a small leather-bound volume of poetry on her lap, when the visitors returned to Gillmore House. Because she was so close to the front entrance, it was no more than polite that she wait to greet the gentlemen.

"Ah, Miss Preston," Zach said upon spying her, a book in her hands and one blue kid slipper peeping from beneath the hem of her blue-sprigged muslin frock. "Well met, ma'am, for I was just asking Peasby to send a maid to find you. I wished your opinion on the horses we brought back from Sir Thomas's stable."

Discarding the little book without a backward glance, Judith joined Zach at the door and allowed him to lead her outside to the carriageway.

"But, sir," she said, upon spying the thoroughbreds, "there are four. Why so many?"

Zach did not answer her question, but put his hand to her back, urging her forward for a better look. "You disapprove my choices, then?"

"No, no," she replied, at the same time silently advising herself to ignore that strong hand between her shoulder blades, and especially to ignore the pleasurable, tingling sensation the hand had induced along her spine. "Who could argue the selection of such beautiful animals?"

Judith nodded a greeting to Lieutenant Gillmore and to the groom who held the reins of the first two horses, then she reached up to stroke the forehead of a powerfully built black gelding that was a full sixteen hands high. After whispering to the animal how regal she thought him, with his neck held high and elegantly arched, she proceeded to a high-spirited bay mare.

"Well ribbed-up," she said, patting the mare's shoulder. "You know your horseflesh, Mr. Camden."

"Undeserved praise, ma'am," the gentleman's brother informed her, "for it is an indisputable fact that a man could wear a blindfold and still choose wisely from Sir Thomas's stables."

When Judith put her fingertips over her mouth to hide her smile, Zach advised her not to bother trying to spare his feelings. "For it is another of those *indisputable* facts, ma'am, that should a person ever begin to think well of himself, there will always be a younger brother only too happy to disabuse him of the notion."

"Zach!" Andrew said, "you are the most complete hand, for you know I did not mean that you—"

"Too late for apologies, sir. The truth will out."

While Andrew and Judith exchanged amused glances, Zach flicked his fingers at the groom, bidding the fellow lead the gelding and the mare aside and allow the other groom to bring his two charges closer.

"And now, Miss Preston," Zach said, "what think you of this little chestnut?"

It was love at first sight for Judith, and as she placed her hands on either side of the filly's cheeks, then blew softly into her nostrils, the animal rewarded her with a gentle whicker of greeting.

"Oh, Zach. She is a darling. But will she bear your weight? I would think the gelding a more suitable mount for a man of your size."

"The black is for me, ma'am. The chestnut is a lady's mount, as is the little dappled gray."

"A lady's . . ." Judith said no more, not certain she could trust herself to speak, not when her throat had grown so uncomfortably tight. *Four horses.* Now the number made sense.

Unaccustomed to receiving unlooked-for kindnesses, and unable to think how to express her appreciation, she put her arms around the filly's neck and pressed her face into the silken mane.

Zach allowed her a moment to compose herself, then he spoke to his brother, his tone teasing. "It has been my experience, Andrew, that the fair sex take an unconscionably long time changing from one outfit to another. Since I know it to be a fool's campaign to impress upon the ladies the need for speed, what say you that if Miss Preston and Miss Lilia keep us waiting much above an hour, we teach them a lesson by riding off without them?"

"Capital idea," Andrew replied.

To Zach's dismay, when Judith let go the horse and turned to him, her eyelashes were suspiciously damp, and she gave him a smile so unexpectedly sincere that it hit him in his midsection with the force of a well-aimed fist.

"Sir," she said, "if you possess a timepiece, you may check it within twenty minutes. At that time, you will find me here, waiting to be tossed into the saddle."

He watched her give the chestnut a final caress then rush inside the house, calling her sister's name as she ran. From the excitement in the lady's voice, a person might be forgiven for thinking he had bestowed upon her some valuable jewel.

Actually, when Zach thought about it, he had purchased a number of quite costly gems over the years, but never had any of the fair recipients appeared so genuinely pleased as had Judith. Nor had they thanked him with such breathtaking smiles.

Nor, he decided some twenty minutes later, when he chanced to turn and see the lady standing in the doorway, her slender person displayed to advantage in a simply cut habit of claret-colored faille, had any of his *cheres amie* ever made him look so forward to an afternoon spent in their company.

Leaving his brother with the horses that had only just returned from the stables where they were saddled and made ready to ride, Zach strolled over to the entrance door. "You are a lady of your word," he said, not bothering to remove the timepiece from his waistcoat pocket.

"And," he added, looking her over from the little jockey hat with its single plume down to the plain leather riding boots that hugged her trim ankles, "what is almost as rare as punctuality, you are a female with sensible taste in riding attire."

To his delight, she chuckled. "What an abominable thing to say."

"Abominable? But I meant it as a tribute."

"Ha! As though any lady below the age of ninety would think it a compliment to be told she wears *sensible* clothing."

"No?" Taking her arm, he led her toward the chestnut. "Pray enlighten me, ma'am, what do ladies below that venerable age wish to be told?"

Judith shrugged her shoulders. "I am but one female, sir. How can I possibly speak for them all?"

After appearing to consider her words for a moment, he put his hand upon his heart and made her an exaggerated bow; when he spoke, it was in a tone dramatic enough for a presentation at King's Theater. "Madam, pray allow me to compliment you upon your raiment. You will surely set a new style among the fashionable."

Judith shook her head. "No, no, sir. Such a fulsome compliment will not do at all. Not for me, you understand, for I am far from fashionable. And since I have not worn this habit anytime these past six years, to remark upon its style is tantamount to offering me an insult."

"Your pardon, ma'am."

Judith watched him stroke his rather angular chin with his thumb and forefinger, as if giving the subject serious thought. "How would it be if I ignored the style of the habit altogether and commented instead upon its color? Perhaps adding some reference to its effect upon your eyes? You know the kind of thing I mean, how it turns them to some jewel or other, like emeralds or sapphires."

"Ordinarily, sir, I should be quite happy to hear such remarks. That is, if I were wearing green or blue. Unfortunately, this color is claret, and I assure you I should not like to be told that my eyes resembled a pair of rubies."

"Madam," he said, as if much put upon, "you are a difficult woman to please."

Judith laughed aloud, and while she was still smiling, he leaned quite close, as if to insure that his words were for her ears only. When he spoke, his voice was just above a whisper. "No man would wish for emeralds or sapphires, fair nymph, not once he had seen what that claret does to the soft ivory of your skin. It casts a sheen upon it, giving it the luster of rare pearls."

Unprepared for the whispered words, or for the breathlessness that assailed her, Judith felt the heat rush to her face.

"Rose-colored pearls," he amended.

"Sir, I—"

"Cousin Lilia!" Andrew called, hurrying toward the vision in azure-blue poplin who stood just inside the doorway.

"Good morning, cousin," she said, looking not at the gentleman but at the riding gloves she was smoothing onto her hands. "It . . . it was kind of you to give my sister and me this outing."

"A pleasure, Cousin Lilia. Though in all honesty, the idea was my brother's."

Judith was happy for the diversion—anything to keep her from further conversation with Zach. To put some distance between herself and him, she stepped over to the chestnut and held her hand out, palm upward, exposing the lump of sugar she had brought. Once the filly gathered the treat with her lips and began to crunch, Judith contented herself with rubbing the animal's velvety forehead.

"You will spoil her," Zach said just behind Judith, startling her with his nearness.

"I beg to differ, sir, for no one has ever been spoiled by a little kindness. Furthermore, it is my belief that there is far too much retribution in this world, and not nearly enough special attention. A little tenderness lets a person— or an animal—know they are important to someone."

What she had said to put that reflective look in his eyes, Judith could not say, and before she had an opportunity to ponder the matter, Lieutenant Gillmore and Lilia approached.

"The gray is yours, Miss Lilia," Zach said. "I understood from young Rainsford that you had ridden her on other occasions."

Zach was not surprised when the innocent remark brought a blush to the damsel's cheeks. What he found most interesting was the look of incredulity upon the face of the young lady's sister.

So, it is as I thought. Judith is unaware that Miss Lilia is a frequent visitor to Rainsford Manor.

Making a mental note to discover her opinion of Sir Thomas and his son, Zach took her arm and led her to the filly's near side, then he locked his fingers together and presented his cupped hands. "Pray allow me to toss you up, Miss Preston."

Judith could not remember the last time she had felt so free. With a marvelous, spirited horse beneath her, the sun upon her back, and the wind upon her face, she felt as if she were one with nature.

By common consent they had chosen the chalk cliffs as their destination, and for some time they had ridden four abreast over the rolling countryside, allowing the horses to gallop. Now, however, as the foursome approached the cliffs, where the land grew rough, and sandy patches and rocks lay ready to trip the unwary, they were obliged to slow the animals to a walk and proceed in single file.

Judith took the lead, breathing deeply of the tangy aroma that filled the air as they neared the channel. So excited was she to reach her destination that she paid little attention to the bright yellow flowers of the sharp-spined gorse, or to the tiny purplish-pink blossoms of the omnipresent heather. Instead, she saved her admiration for the white sea campion that clung to the rock surfaces almost as if in defiance of the harsh environment. At her first glimpse of the little flowers, Judith smiled, fancying they had clung there all these months, waiting for her return.

In a matter of seconds, she was at the cliff's edge, gasping at the sudden, sharp drop to the channel, almost as if she had never seen the view before. Fifty feet below, the blue-green waves lapped against the silver gray sands, while above, the cloudless blue sky seemed to reach into eternity.

Hearing the *clop-clop* of hooves just behind her, and knowing somehow that it was the gelding, she waited for Zach to draw up alongside her. "I had almost forgotten how glorious it is here."

"Truly magnificent," he agreed. "Though a bit noisy."

As though only just noticing the raucous cries of the birds, Judith put her hand to her forehead to shield her eyes from the glare of the sun reflected off the white chalk face of the cliffs. Scanning the area, she said, "The various colonies of birds return each year to build their nests in the rocks, and to fish the waters. When I was a child, I fancied the creatures were calling out to one another, gossiping like neighbors returned from a long journey."

"So, you came here often?"

She nodded. "Papa Albert brought us. He loved it. He knew the proper names for all the cliff dwellers, and even had a special name for one or two of the old-timers who came back year after year."

She pointed to a flock of gull-like birds that seemed to boomerang around the cliffs, their blue-gray wings straight and stiff. "Do you see those? They are called fulmars."

For a moment, Zach looked where she pointed, but almost immediately his attention was drawn upward, higher and higher, where a number of soaring birds rode the updraughts that were produced when the wind from the sea collided with the cliffs. "And those?" he asked.

"Kittiwakes. Listen for a moment, and you can hear them call their name."

He listened obediently, then he pointed toward the water where numerous smaller birds dove for fish. "And what of those crook-necked fellows? The ones with the bottle-green plumage and the funny crests."

"That is the shag. He and his cousin, the cormorant, spend hours chasing the fish underwater, then afterwards they like to perch upon the rocks and stretch out their wings to dry."

"And that creature there?" He pointed down the stretch of beach where a lone rider astride a handsome bay trotted toward them. "Have you a name for him as well?"

Judith shaded her eyes again, the better to see the rider. "Why, I believe that is Stan Rainsford," she said, surprise in her voice. "How very odd to chance upon him here. Of all places he might have ridden, I wonder what can have prompted him to journey to the cliffs."

"Hmm," Zach murmured. "What, indeed?"

Six

It was a good quarter of an hour before young Mr. Rainsford reached the foursome from Gillmore House. And if
he had been unfriendly toward Andrew earlier while in the
stables of Rainsford Manor, he was downright churlish
when encountering the lieutenant riding beside Miss Lilia.

Having discarded his workman's clothing for a well-cut
coat of blue superfine and biscuit-colored pantaloons, the
young man appeared every inch a gentleman. Doffing his
beaver to the ladies, he said, "Miss Preston. Miss Lilia."
For the two gentlemen, he spared scarcely a nod.

"Stan," Lilia said, her English rose complexion gone
pale as the chalk cliffs, "why are you here?"

"No reason," he replied, staring at Andrew in a manner
reminiscent of a dog come to guard a bone. "Just thought
I would take a little ride."

"If this is a *little* ride," Andrew said, "I should jolly well
like to see what you call a long one, for we have been gone
this hour and more, and Cousin Lilia—"

"Rainsford," Zach interrupted before his brother unwit-
tingly pushed the younger man past his point of endurance,
"as it happens, I am more than happy to welcome you to
our party, for Miss Preston and I were just discussing the
possibility of a race on the beach."

Ignoring the look of total surprise upon Judith's face at

this piece of news, he continued. "And since Andrew is obviously tired from the *long* ride, and Miss Lilia was saying only a few minutes ago that she would like to dismount for a short rest, I was at a loss as to what to do. However, now that you are here, I know you will not mind remaining here for half an hour or so to keep these two young cousins company."

If Zach felt the least shame for having put words into the mouths of all three of his companions, his face did not show it. Not waiting for Stan's reply, he caught the filly's bridle and turned her in the direction of the path Mr. Rainsford had used to reach them, and without so much as a *by-your-leave,* he led Judith away.

Good manners, and a very steep incline, kept the lady quiet until they reached the beach, but once they were on even terrain, she gave vent to her anger. "At what moment, sir, did I become a marionette and you the puppeteer?"

"I beg your pardon?"

"As well you might, though I collect that was not an apology but a ruse to convince me that you have no idea to what I refer."

"But, ma'am, I assure you—"

"Spare me any of your assurances. After the way you just manipulated the four of us, the very least you can do is not insult my intelligence by a recitation of your supposed innocence."

Far from taking offense, he smiled. "As reprehensible as my actions may have appeared, I wish you will trust me that all was done for the best."

"A quote, I believe, from Ghengis Khan."

This time, he laughed outright. "Does this mean you are too angry to pit your horsemanship against mine?"

Judith was sorely tempted to deal him the rebuff he deserved, but the thought of a gallop across the sand was more of a temptation than she could withstand . . . that and the way Zach's eyes crinkled at the corners when he laughed, making him appear younger and even more of a rogue than . . .

For the love of Heaven! Turn away. Do not dwell upon the scoundrel's handsome face!

Advising herself not to be any more of a fool than she could help, Judith pointed to a spot about a quarter of a mile down the beach—a spot where a row of puffins perched upon a tree limb that had washed up on the sand. "Do you see those birds with the gray and orange beaks?"

He nodded.

"Their resting place is our destination. Agreed?"

"As you wish. Any rules or restrictions?"

"None, sir. As a matter of fact, you have my permission to try every dirty trick in the book, for you will have need of them if you are to best me."

"Oh, ho, Miss Brass Face! Such an arrogant boast begs a wager."

For a woman who vehemently disapproved of gaming, Judith's reply came quickly, requiring less than a moment's thought. "A million pounds, sir, for the winner."

Zach's eyebrows lifted. "A formidable wager. You will forgive my impertinence, but I question your ability to pay such a sum should you not prove the victor. Therefore, if *I* am expected to risk my money, I should like to know what will be my reward if you lose."

"It makes no difference to me," she replied airily. "You may name what you will."

"Anything?" The light in his eyes was positively devilish. "Madam, I call that a dangerous piece of overconfidence, for who knows what I might demand in payment."

After lowering her eyelids in spurious humility, Judith said, "I pray, sir, that my belief in my own ability has not given you a disgust of me." Then, with a chuckle, "And I apologize in advance for the sand my horse will throw in your face as she gallops across the finish line."

"Ooh, Judith," he drawled, "now you have gone too far. I had meant to do the gentlemanly thing and let you win, but now, you must see that is impossible. No man could—"

"Let me win! Of all the puffed-up, conceited . . ."

She stopped, unable to think of a word scathing enough; then, without warning, she yanked off her jockey hat and slapped it across the filly's flank. The chestnut's response was everything Judith could have hoped for, and within seconds the animal was flying down the stretch of beach, leaping and bounding as though there really were a million pounds wagered upon the outcome of the race.

Above the sound of the filly's hooves, pounding upon the hard-packed sand, Judith heard the outraged screeching of the myriad of cliff dwellers disturbed by the sudden appearance of a giant, galloping beast. She spared neither time nor thought for the birds' justifiable anger; instead, she leaned close to the chestnut's neck, pushing her foot down hard in the stirrup iron so that she was able to lift herself an inch or two above the saddle.

Not for the first time in her life, Judith wished she might ride astride, with both feet planted firmly in the stirrups, and without the restraint of several yards of billowing skirt. If only she could ride thus, she would show her opponent some real speed.

Spurring the filly to try even harder, Judith felt the wind whip at her face, yanking her hair from its knot and blowing it all about her head. At one point, she was uncertain if the hair that veiled her eyes belonged to her or to the chestnut's mane.

With her destination and sweet victory mere yards away, Judith stole a glance to her right. To her surprise, Zach and the gelding were mere inches off her pace. Like her, Zach was posting, and also like her, he was traveling very fast.

Ordinarily, Judith would have had the advantage in a race, for she was several stone lighter than her opponent, but Zach was stronger than she and his horse was much more powerful than the filly. To Judith's dismay, just before they reached the startled puffins, the gelding surged ahead, gaining upon the filly by a nose. By a head. By a neck!

There was not the least doubt as to who was first to cross the finish line.

They rode some distance beyond the water-logged tree limb, gradually slowing the horses to a trot, then to a walk, allowing the winded animals to catch their breath and cool down. As for the humans, Judith was still breathing hard when Zach dismounted and came to her, reaching his hands up to her waist to help her from the saddle.

"First," she said, putting her hands on his wrists to stop him from lifting her down, "tell me what I am to forfeit. What will you seek in payment for your triumph?"

Zach stood quite still, his hands almost circling her slim waist, and looked up into her gamine's face. Her usually neat hair was in glorious disarray, the medium-brown tresses wind-tossed and falling all about her shoulders, and her eyes were bright with the excitement of the race. Her soft, full lips were slightly parted, and as she breathed in through her mouth, Zach knew without question what he meant to collect as his reward.

"I am tempted," he said, "to take my 'winnings' from your lips."

A quick, nearly inaudible gasp was her only response.

"A kiss," he said softly. "A small forfeiture, surely, for one who bade me name my own prize."

He gave her several moments to say nay, if that was her wish, but she said nothing. She merely stared at him, and though her big blue eyes exhibited uncertainty, they showed neither fright nor refusal.

When Judith felt Zach begin to lift her slowly from the saddle, she leaned toward him, resting her hands upon his upper arms, an action that put their faces mere inches apart. She thought he might claim his kiss then and there, and when he did not, she ceased to breathe.

At that moment, however, being deprived of air seemed a small price to pay for the excitement that coursed through her veins at the warmth of his hands upon her waist, and the feel of those rock-hard muscles beneath her fingers.

Judith's heart all but leapt from her chest when he held her aloft, then slowly brought her close to him—so close she could feel the round brass buttons of his waistcoat press against her bosom. As if not wishing to rush the moment, he took his time before gradually allowing her feet to touch the ground.

Immeasurable time passed as they stood thus, unmoving, yet gazing at one another, with Judith lost in his cool gray eyes—lost with no wish to be found. She was alive with an excitement she had never felt before—an awareness that set her lips on fire and made her ache to know the secrets of a kiss.

Zach seemed to understand what she wanted, and he had just begun to lower his head to hers when a large white-winged gull dove perilously close to them. The point of the bird's powerful, pale yellow bill just missed Zach's ear, and its shrill, nerve-wracking *pee-ol* of alarm made the two humans jump apart. Unfortunately, they were not the only ones startled by the cry. The chestnut took instant exception to such behavior and began to side-step out of harm's way.

Everything happened very quickly. First came the screech of the gull, then the filly's nervous movement, followed by Judith's surprised cry, which frightened the animal even more. As Zach grabbed the horse's bridle to keep her from bolting, Judith screamed again, for something had hold of her skirt and was pulling it with such force it threatened to yank her legs out from under her.

With her arms flailing like the wings of a newly fledged bird, she managed to keep from falling, and when she turned to see who or what had threatened her, she found the hem of her habit caught fast in the stirrup iron. As luck would have it, before she could pull the material free, the gull made a second dive, frightening the filly into attempting to break free of Zach's hold.

This time, when the horse sidestepped, Judith could not withstand the pull. Like a hapless animal caught in a hunter's snare, she felt the material tighten like a noose around her legs. An instant later, her feet were snatched from beneath her.

She landed on her side, her right shoulder hitting the ground first, then her head. As the frightened filly dragged her several feet across the rough sand, Judith felt the moist grains grating against her cheek. Blessedly, the fall had knocked the breath from her lungs, and while she gasped for air, blackness descended. As she drifted into unconsciousness, the last thing she heard was Zach's voice.

"Whoa!" he called. "Whoa, girl. Steady."

From the corner of his eye, Zach saw Judith pitch forward, and for a split second he thought to let go of the horse's bridle and run to help her up. Fortunately, before he could act upon that plan, he realized that the skirt of her habit had somehow become entangled with the stirrup iron, and that she was being dragged across the sand.

Aghast at what had happened, and terrified that Judith might be dragged even further by the frightened horse, or worse yet, trampled beneath the filly's lethal hooves, Zach threw his arms around the chestnut's neck and held on with all his strength. Meanwhile, the horse tossed her powerful head back and forth in a bid for freedom, her eyes rolling in fear and her ears laid back in anger.

For several minutes they struggled, with Zach gasping for breath, yet talking the entire time, saying whatever came into his mind, his purpose to reassure the animal that all was well. Finally, Zach prevailed and the horse grew relatively calm.

Not fully convinced by the filly's exhibited submissiveness, Zach did not release her immediately. Still worried she might bolt, he grasped the thick chestnut mane with one hand, all the while gently stroking the animal's neck with the other and crooning softly to her. Continuing thus, he inched his way closer to the stirrup and the captured skirt hem.

He saw the problem immediately. The saddle, having come from Lord Gillmore's tack room, was far from new, and the arch of the stirrup iron had worn through, leaving a break at the juncture of the arch and the bottom bar that was not visible until weight was put on the stirrup. The hem of Judith's skirt must have become wedged in the break while she was posting.

Keeping his fingers firmly entwined in the filly's mane, Zach put his boot in the stirrup and pressed down just hard enough to separate the metal. With the arch and the bar no longer joined, it was the work of a minute to free the claret faille and let the hem fall to the ground beside Judith's booted feet.

After carefully pushing the horse out of the way, lest she grow frightened again and step on the fallen rider, Zach knelt down beside a very pale, very still Judith. He put his fingers to her neck to feel for a pulse, and to his relief, the beat was strong and regular.

"Judith," he called quietly. "Judith, can you hear me?"

She muttered something he did not understand, then she opened her eyes and looked up at him, blinking several times before finally focusing her gaze upon his face. "The filly?" she asked.

Zach exhaled noisily, feeling as if he breathed for the first time since he saw Judith go down. "The horse is fine. It is *your* health which concerns me. Can you tell me where you hurt?"

"If you wish," she said, making a feeble attempt at a smile. "Though I am convinced it would be quicker if I related to you those one or two areas of my anatomy that are *not* throbbing with pain."

When she tried to sit up, he quickly put his hand to her shoulder to stop her, instructing her in no uncertain terms to remain still. "Before I allow you to move about, I must see if anything is broken." Then, in a softer tone, "I promise not to add to your pain any more than is necessary."

"I know you will not," she said. "Do whatever you feel you must."

Carefully and methodically, Zach touched every accessible bone in her body, and only after the examination was completed, and she had not cried out at any time, did he help her to sit up.

"Here," he said, removing a clean, white linen handkerchief from his pocket, "let me wipe your face a little."

Sitting on the sand beside her, he took her chin between his thumb and forefinger and gently dabbed away the moist grains that had adhered to her cheek. "The skin is not broken, thank Heaven, but you have a most impressive abrasion. I do not scruple to inform you that it will burn prodigiously when next it comes into contact with soap and water."

While he had administered to her, Judith had looked directly at him, not in the least embarrassed. However, at his words, she suddenly turned bright pink and raised unsteady hands to her wind-tousled tresses.

"Oh, my," she said, feeling the unbound hair that seemed to fly in all directions at once. "I . . . I must appear a perfect fright."

"Too missish by half," he said, his voice so gentle it was almost a caress. "After all, what is a little wind and sand to a wood nymph?"

With his forefinger still beneath her chin, he pushed upward gently, urging her to look at him again. "You appear exactly what you are, Doe Eyes, a thoroughly entrancing creature."

Seven

"I assure you," Judith said, "it is but the slightest of headaches, and not at all serious enough to preclude my riding alone."

"Nevertheless," Zach said, "we shall ride together."

"Indeed, sir, there is no need, for I shall do famously once you help me to my feet."

Zach offered no response this time, but continued his inspection of the gelding's tack, assuring himself that no other mishaps were likely to befall them. When he was satisfied that all was in order, he turned and walked back to where he had left Judith, still sitting upon the sand.

"The filly is just there," she said, pointing a little way down the beach where the chestnut stood, her reins dragging on the ground. "Perhaps you should catch her first, then come back to assist me."

Zach did not even glance at that spot where Judith pointed. "End of discussion," he said, then he bent down, scooped her up in his arms, and lifted her off the sand.

After the initial shock of being subjected to an act of such familiarity, Judith surrendered to the inevitable and let Zach take her where he would. Actually, she was not as annoyed by his high-handedness as she might have been; a result, no doubt, of her still feeling the effects of the accident—that and the sudden erratic pounding of her heart. Once she had made up her mind not to protest Zach's behavior, she found it amazingly easy to slide her arms over his broad shoulders and snuggle her head against his neck.

Though Judith had never before been carried in a man's arms, she decided it was a thoroughly delightful mode of transportation, and one she would not have missed for the world. To feel Zach's strength, to be held close to his heart, to be allowed to put her arms around him, was such an exhilarating experience that she wished it might continue for a long time.

To her disappointment, the pleasurable episode lasted mere seconds, for Zach needed only a half dozen long, purposeful strides to reach the waiting gelding, where he set Judith on the front of the saddle. Before she could bemoan the loss of Zach's warmth, however, he put his foot in the stirrup, swung his leg over the horse's back, and settled into the padded leather just behind her.

Immediately, the situation improved, for Zach wrapped his strong arm around her waist, pulling her close against his chest to insure her safety, then he bid her rest her head against his shoulder. Needing no further encouragement, Judith acquiesced, and sighing with contentment she closed her eyes, letting him find his way back up the path as best he could.

When they reached the cliff top several minutes later, they found Lilia, Stan, and Andrew on their hands and knees like children at play, looking over the cliff's edge, eagerly searching for fossils buried in the limestone. Since the exploration was a rather noisy one, requiring shouted advice from Andrew to, "Look but an inch farther to your right," and from Stan to, "See what you make of that yellowish shell just there," the three young people did not immediately realize that Judith and Zach had returned.

Only when the gelding approached the threesome did Judith become embarrassed by her present situation, realizing how fast she must appear to onlookers, riding double with a gentleman and snuggled contentedly against his chest.

Of course, she need not have been concerned. One look at her dishevelled hair, the rent in the hem of her habit, and the worried look upon Zach's face, and any but the veryest clodpole could deduce what had happened.

Lilia was the first to speak. "Judith!" she screamed, scrambling to her feet and running toward her sister, "you are injured."

"Miss Preston has taken a nasty fall," Zach replied.

"Sir," Mr. Rainsford said, coming forward, his arms outstretched as if ready to receive the lady if that was Zach's wish. "Shall I take her?"

"I think not. We have achieved a certain balance that is best left undisturbed. However," he added, "I hope you can supply me with the information I desire."

The youthful face beneath the sandy blond hair was at odds with the lad's serious expression. "I am at your disposal, sir."

"Good man. I do not believe Miss Preston should be taxed further by riding all the way back to Gillmore House, and since you are the person most familiar with the area, I wonder if you know of some place close by where she might rest. Also, can you tell me where I may find a physician to examine her?"

"There is a cottage less than a mile from here," Stan replied. "It is the home of Abel Wimmer, a yeoman farmer, and I am certain Miss Preston can be made comfortable there while I ride to Blinbourne for the apothecary." He paused for a moment, his face pink with embarrassment.

"Forgive me, sir, but the chestnut . . . is she injured? Have I time to fetch her before we leave?"

"The filly is unharmed," Zach replied. "As for fetching her, I believe you may trust my brother to see to that task."

Lieutenant Gillmore was halfway to his own mount before his brother finished the statement. "Shall I bring the animal to the farmer's cottage?"

Zach shook his head. "Convey her to the stables at Gillmore House, then have his lordship's coachman put a team to my chaise and bring it to the cottage."

"And what of Mrs. Gillmore?" Andrew asked. "What shall I tell her?"

Before Zach could reply, Miss Lilia made her presence felt. "If you please, Cousin Andrew, tell my mother that I will not leave Judith's side until we are returned to her. She knows she may trust me to do all that is needed."

If the two brothers were surprised to witness this evidence of maturity in the young lady, not so Mr. Rainsford. That gentleman merely tossed Lilia up onto the dappled gray mare then mounted his own bay gelding. "Follow me, Mr. Camden," he said. "I shall have you at the cottage in a trice."

The ride was not accomplished in a trice, but it needed only slightly more than ten minutes before they reached Abel Wimmer's farm. The fields were well tended and prosperous looking, and at the moment they were filled with row upon row of maturing flax that would soon turn the area into a sea of blue.

Giving little attention to the fields, the party rode up the lane until they crossed over the little arched stone bridge that led to the house. It was a charming two-story cottage, whose stone was weathered to a deep honey-gold, and at his first sight of it, Zach breathed a sigh of relief, for it appeared both homey and inviting.

A neat low hedge, liberally entwined with tendrils of purplish tufted vetch, separated the side garden from the lane. It was at the wooden gate that gave access through the hedge that they met the farmer's wife, a pretty young matron with blond braids and apple cheeks.

"Mary," Stan said the instant they reached the gate, "I believe you know Miss Preston and Miss Lilia Gillmore. The gentleman is—"

"Please," she bade him, making a quick assessment of what had happened, "let us dispense with the formalities for the moment." She looked up at Zach, who still held Judith before him. "Bring the lady inside, sir. We'll put her in the front chamber, for there is plenty of light there."

Though Judith declared herself perfectly able to walk, and asked to be set down, Zach turned a deaf ear to her plea. Dismounting quickly, he lifted her from the gelding, then he scooped her up in his arms before she had time to protest. At the same time, their hostess gave the toddler she held to the maid-of-all-work and shooed a rambunctious lad of about five years of age to the back of the garden to play.

After unlatching the gate, she said, "This way, sir," then she ushered them inside the cottage and up the narrow, carpeted steps that led to the six upper-story bedchambers.

Less than an hour later, Stan returned to the cottage with the apothecary, Mr. Autry, a rail-thin, nervous-looking man of about thirty years. Having envisioned an avuncular old gentleman with silver hair, Zach was suddenly reluctant to put Judith into the apothecary's care.

Sensing his apprehension, Mary Wimmer assured him that he need feel no concern. "Mr. Autry has already seen our sons through a battery of childhood complaints, and I have complete faith in his ability."

She gave Zach a moment to assimilate the information before she spoke again. "Now, sir, if you and the young lady would be so kind as to step belowstairs, so that Mr. Autry might examine Miss Preston in privacy, I will advise you both the moment you may return." She smiled to soften the incivility of ordering them from the room. "If I know our Hannah, she will have taken some refreshments to the parlor. Perhaps Miss Lilia would find a cup of Bohea refreshing."

Perceiving the wisdom of their hostess's suggestion, Zach did as he was bid and escorted Lilia to the small, neat parlor where Stan stood gazing out the front window. A tea tray had, indeed, been taken to the room, and Zach instructed the younger man to pour Lilia a cup. As for himself, he did not think he could swallow anything until he was certain that Judith had sustained no permanent injury.

Needing a breath of air, he slipped past the wooden door that stood open and through the side garden, not stopping until he reached the little arched bridge where a crystal clear brook flowed swiftly toward the south. The water was no more than a foot deep, but recalling that even shallow water could prove hazardous to small children, Zach retraced his steps and made certain the gate was securely latched.

"Hello," said a small voice from the back of the garden.

Looking in the direction of the voice, Zach spied Master Jeremy Wimmer, who was a small, masculine copy of his blond, blue-eyed mother. At the moment, the child sat quietly upon a wooden bench, the spot shaded by a trellis twined about by Convolvulus on the verge of displaying its pink blossoms. If the light in the boy's eyes was anything to go by, however, sitting quietly in the shade was not his usual occupation.

"Hello," Zach replied.

"Do you wish to have a turn with my top, sir? It hums as it spins."

"Does it, now? I should call that a top worth having."

Obviously much struck by this surprisingly discerning assessment from an adult, the five-year-old slid to the end of the bench, offering the remainder for the guest's comfort, while preserving a few inches of the hard surface upon which to spin the top.

Zach took the proffered seat, stretching his long legs before him and crossing his booted feet at the ankles.

Though busy with his toy, Master Wimmer spared a moment to eye the visitor from head to toe. "I shall be quite tall one day," he said.

"A wise decision," Zach said. "It makes fetching things off high shelves so much easier."

A corner of the neat garden was given over to herbs, and Zach breathed deeply of some delicate, minty fragrance he could not quite identify. He supposed it was either basil or heartmint, but whatever it was, he found it soothing. Wondering if he might be forgiven for stealing a sprig to take up to Judith, he was surprised to discover that the little boy had asked him a question and was patiently waiting for a reply.

"I beg your pardon, lad. I was woolgathering. What did you say?"

"Is your wife very sick?"

"The lady is not ill. She fell. And she is not my wife. Merely a friend."

"Oh." After a reflective moment, the boy said, "Where is your wife?"

"I have none."

At this piece of information, the child's eyes grew round as saucers. "But you must have, for you are all grown up."

Zach felt suspiciously as though he had been tried and found wanting. But how could he explain to a child that he had never met a woman he would like to marry? Had not, in fact, ever met one he could tolerate for more than a few hours at a time. Though beautiful women were always available when a man had wealth—even a few with both beauty and brains—Zach had never found a woman he respected enough to offer her his hand in marriage.

"Papa says a good wife makes life worth living, and that when I grow up, I shall definitely want one. Though," the child added, "I won't have Betty Sams, no matter what, for she pushed me down and took my new whistle."

"Very wise, my boy. By all means, I think you should find a lass who does not push or steal."

As for a wife making life worth living, Zach kept to himself his doubts upon that subject.

Thinking he had given the apothecary ample time to examine Judith, Zach excused himself to Master Wimmer then strolled back into the house. The carpet softened the sound of his footfalls, and just outside the parlor, he paused, debating whether to make his presence known to Miss Lilia and Rainsford, or to continue up the stairs. It was while he waited that he heard the two young people in conversation.

"He wanted two hundred pounds," Mr. Rainsford said, "and he wanted it up front. Before promising his services."

Lilia gasped. "Two hundred pounds! So much?"

Zach could not believe the apothecary had demanded such an exorbitant sum to come out to see to Judith's injuries, but if he had, it was not up to young Rainsford to stand the nonsense, and Zach would tell him so immediately.

He had turned to enter the parlor when the young man's next words halted his step.

"And, of course, there is the matter of the silks, the paddock fees, and the entrance money. The whole should come to about eight hundred pounds."

"Oh, Stan. What are we to do?"

"I do not know, my love. I had hoped to defer the payments until after Stanbury's Bess had won the race, but now I see I have much to learn about the business of horse racing."

My love? It was the term of endearment that most caught Zach's attention. As for the horse race, he found nothing startling in that, for the young man owned a filly who met the qualifications for next week's heat. What could be more understandable than his wanting to test the animal's mettle?

Miss Lilia began to cry softly. "I shall be forced to marry my cousin."

"Never! I shall find some way to prevent it."

The young lady sniffed. "But how? If you do not enter the race, then how can you win the prize money? And if you do not win the prize, then how are we to pay for our elopement? And how shall we live once we are wed? Your birthday wants another seven months, and until you reach your majority, you may not touch the money left you by your grandfather."

She began to cry in earnest. "If only Sir Thomas were not so ambitious for you."

Mr. Rainsford must have taken her in his arms, for her sobs had a muffled sound, as if her face were buried against the gentleman's shoulder. " 'Tis foolish, indeed," he said, "for my father to think I might marry some young lady of exalted birth. Not that I wish to, of course, for I have never wanted anyone but you! But ever since Father was knighted, he has thought of nothing but gaining an entrée to society."

Having heard enough of their conversation to put two and two together with a fair degree of accuracy, Zach backed away from the door and stepped lightly upon the stairs. So, he had been correct in his assessment of Rainsford's feelings toward Miss Lilia. As for the young lady, she must fancy herself in love as well, or she would not be contemplating such a socially unacceptable step as an elopement.

Not that their alliance would be so very unsuitable. Though far from a brilliant match, it was hardly contemptible. Miss Lilia might possess no marriage portion, but she was a real beauty and the granddaughter of a baron. As for Mr. Rainsford, he was well educated and honorable, and his father's wealth must make up in part for his lack of social connections.

Wondering how much of this overheard conversation he dared tell Judith, Zach continued up the stairs and knocked at the door to the front bedchamber.

"Sir," Mary Wimmer said, opening the door wide and inviting him to enter, "you have arrived in good time. Mr. Autry has only just completed his examination, and he has given us the happy news that Miss Preston sustained no serious injuries."

More relieved than he would have thought possible, Zach looked across the room to the large, heavily carved walnut bed where Judith had been tucked up beneath a pretty striped quilt. Several pillows had been placed behind her back, and in lieu of the claret habit, she now wore a modest wrapper of opaque Irish linen—a wrapper whose only adornment was the little white satin ribbons that held the garment together at the neck and across the front.

"Just a number of bruises," the apothecary added to Mary's report. "As for any resulting stiffness, I have left a liniment that should prove beneficial. Of course, if Miss

Preston will be led by me, she will avail herself of a few days' bed rest."

Judith thanked the man, then she looked meaningfully at Zach, as if to convey to him what she thought of the suggestion that she should play the part of an invalid. "If anyone would like to hear *my* opinion as to what would prove beneficial," she said, "I should cast my vote for that tea Mrs. Wimmer mentioned earlier."

Zach indicated that Mr. Autry should precede him through the door, then just before they quit the room, he glanced back at Judith. "I shall bring you a cup."

"And an almond tart, please," she said, "with gobs of clotted cream."

When Zach raised a questioning eyebrow, she smiled impishly. "Mrs. Wimmer says Hannah has a way with tarts, and I have not eaten since early this morning."

Happy to know that she had an appetite, Zach inclined his head, as if in obedience to her request. "With our hostess's permission, I will see that a tray is prepared."

After he escorted the apothecary to his carriage and paid him for his services, Zach returned to the parlor to see about a tray for Judith, only to discover that Lilia had taken one up several minutes earlier.

"Wanted to see for herself that Miss Preston is on the mend," Stan informed him.

Allowing the sisters time for a private visit, Zach spent a half hour with Mr. Rainsford, discovering by means of a series of subtle questions that the young man had no social ambitions whatsoever.

"I should be content," he said, "never to set foot outside Dorset. I wish to breed and train thoroughbreds, and aside from that goal, I want what every man wants—a partner I can love and respect, and Heaven willing, a few children to share our lives."

Another young man desirous of finding a wife! Zach decided there must be something in the Dorset air.

Still, he liked young Rainsford, and if he could further the lad's cause in any way, he would do so. And not just because it ran parallel to his own desire to see his brother leave Gillmore House without the encumbrance of a fiancée.

When Lilia joined them several minutes later, Zach excused himself and went up to see if there was anything Judith needed. Stopping just inside the open doorway, he leaned his shoulder against the jamb and studied the freshfaced young woman in the ornate bed. Someone, her sister perhaps, had brushed the tangles from Judith's hair. The thick, dark tresses had then been tied at the nape of her neck with a length of pink ribbon, and the whole brought forward to rest upon the lady's right shoulder.

Not since his boyhood days had Zach yanked a hair ribbon, but at that moment he felt the strongest urge to do so once again. He wanted to sit on the edge of that large, roomy bed and free Judith's hair, letting the shiny satin billow about her shoulders. He wanted to run his fingers through—

"No," she said, putting an end to his licentious daydream—a fantasy he had no right to entertain and one she would certainly not appreciate, "you are very kind, but I do not need a thing. As a matter of fact, I have been so well looked after, that I wonder you do not warn me against becoming spoiled."

He smiled in acknowledgement of her sally. "My earlier warning was in reference to your spoiling the filly. Young ladies are a different matter altogether."

"A very liberal view, sir."

"Madam, I am a very liberal man."

Judith was not certain how she should reply to such banter, for her wits seemed rather dull at the moment. As Zach stood there in the doorway, looking relaxed and self-assured, it needed all Judith's concentration just to keep her gaze from lingering over-long on his muscular person.

Never mind that his cream-colored pantaloons were irrevocably stained by the sand, or that his battle with the filly had caused the left shoulder of his Devonshire brown coat to come unsewn; Judith thought him every inch the gentleman . . . every inch the hero . . . and quite the handsomest man she had ever seen.

"I have drunk a bracing cup of Bohea," she informed him, "and eaten an almond tart literally swimming in clotted cream. Now, all that remains to be wished for is the return of the maid who promised to rub some of the apothecary's rather noxious-smelling liniment on my tender spots."

Zach smiled wickedly. "No need to trouble the servant, ma'am. I would be happy to perform that service for you."

Though Judith knew she should rebuke him for such an improper suggestion, she chuckled instead. "Thank you, sir, but I believe I shall wait for the maid."

Apparently encouraged by her forbearance, Zach made a second recommendation. "When I was a lad, I was cared for by an elderly nursemaid who held both physicians and *materia medica* in great disdain, believing they did children more harm than good. As a result of her stringently held bias, the woman employed a rather simple curative for most childhood cuts and scrapes. Upon each injury she would place a kiss guaranteed to make it better."

He did not look at Judith, but straightened his sadly crushed cravat, paying special attention to the arrangement of the folds. "If you should wish me to try what that *kiss-*

it-to-make-it-better treatment would do for you, I am agreeable. Purely in the interest of science, you understand."

Though Judith felt the heat rush to her cheeks, she did not look away. "You are all goodness, sir, to present me with an opportunity to aid in the advancement of science. However, considering what befell me the last time you were so generous as to offer to kiss me, I think I would do better to place my reliance upon the liniment."

He sighed. "As you wish, madam. But should you change your mind at some later date, I am willing to give the nursemaid's regimen a try."

"Sir," she said, "you are a true humanitarian."

Eight

As it transpired, Judith remained at Wimmer Cottage for the next four days, with her sister and her mother making daily visits to her, their objective to keep her spirits up while she obeyed the apothecary's advice for bed rest.

Though Zach insisted the ladies avail themselves of his chaise, he did not intrude upon the family party. Instead, he contented himself with sending along such unexceptional items as he thought Judith might find amusing: a book of poetry the first day, a drawing pad and pencils the second day, a collection of accrostics and puzzles on the third day.

Because searching out these little gifts required a visit to the village, Zach and Andrew formed the habit of riding to Blinbourne each morning. After remaining for a nuncheon at the Dancing Bear, where every snatch of overheard conversation centered on the race meet that was still several days away, they rode about the countryside for most of the afternoon, their purpose to stay away from Gillmore House for as many hours as possible. Had they cared to know it, their long absences irritated his lordship past endurance.

"Damnation!" Lord Gillmore shouted when Peasby returned to the drawing room Monday afternoon to inform his master that the heir was from home once again. "The fortnight is half over, and we are no closer to an understanding about the wedding then we were the first day the young jackanapes arrived. How am I to have a talk with the fellow if he is forever gadding about in this ramshackled manner?"

"I am sure I cannot say, milord."

The old gentleman glared at his butler. "He is an insolent young pup! He knows I am desirous of speaking privately with him, yet he keeps me waiting as though he cared not a fig for my wishes. And do not think I cannot see the hand of that curst brother of his in this Turkish treatment. If only I could be rid of the fellow."

"The lieutenant?"

"No, imbecile! The brother."

The present conversation, far from calming his lordship, caused him to grow more irritable. Looking about him for something upon which to vent his spleen, he grabbed up the pewter tankard Peasby had just set upon the small table beside the leather wing chair. Uttering a string of oaths that would have made a seaman blush, Lord Gillmore flung the vessel against the stone hearth. It bounced off the stone and rolled across the room, spilling a trail of warm ale upon the handsome red-and-blue Axminster carpet.

While Peasby signaled the footman to attend to the spill, his lordship continued to rant. "I shall be rid of the interfering rogue! By Heaven I will! And once the brother is out of the way, I will bring my heir to a realization of the respect that is due me as head of the family. He shall marry my granddaughter. And right soon! Or he will not see a groat of my money, not as long as I have breath in my lungs."

Peasby cleared his throat. "Forgive me, milord, but how is such a thing to be arranged? As you know, Mr. Camden scarcely leaves the lieutenant's side from one minute to the next."

Lord Gillmore thought the matter through for a time. After several minutes, he smiled—if the slight upturn of the thin lips in that gaunt face could be called a smile. "I have it."

Peasby and the footman exchanged looks.

"Send for Miss Preston," Lord Gillmore ordered. " 'Tis time that insolent chit earned her keep."

"But, milord," Peasby replied, "Miss Preston is still at Wimmer Cottage. Surely you remember, sir, that the young lady met with an accident."

Lord Gillmore banged his cane upon the hearth. "Drat the chit! Been eating her head off at my expense for a twelvemonth, and now that I have need of her, she chooses to have an accident."

The butler waited until his master had calmed down, then he said, "I believe Mrs. Gillmore was to bring her daughter home this afternoon."

"Good. The moment they arrive, send the girl to me."

Peasby cleared his throat meaningfully. "Milord, do you not think that Miss Preston will desire to rest after her journey?"

"Rest! Been resting for several days." Then, as if thinking aloud, he muttered, "Too bad she's got none of my granddaughter's beauty. An odd-looking chit, if you ask me, but I suppose there's no help for it. Beggars cannot be choosers."

"Sir? I do not understand—"

"You do not need to understand. Just send the chit to me, I tell you. She is the very one to keep that rascal busy while I speak with my heir."

It was the next morning before Zach saw Judith. Upon her return to Gillmore House from Wimmer Cottage, she had gone directly to her room, and that evening she had chosen to take her dinner abovestairs. She was joined in that activity by her mother and her sister, and as a consequence, the three gentlemen had partaken of a hostessless and rather strained meal, after which the brothers took themselves off to the Dancing Bear for a nightcap.

Zach had hoped to see Judith at breakfast. In that goal he was doomed to failure, for when he found the morning room empty and asked Peasby if Miss Preston had come down yet, the butler informed him that the lady was in the bookroom with his lordship.

"Miss Preston? With Lord Gillmore?"

"Yes, sir. His lordship wanted to speak with Miss Preston when she arrived yesterday, but Mrs. Gillmore forbade it, saying her daughter was in need of quiet."

"Good for Mrs. Gillmore."

"That's as may be, sir. But as you can imagine, his lordship was not pleased to be kept waiting."

"Threw a tantrum, did he?"

"Yes, sir. And also the silver epergne that used to sit on the sideboard in the dining room."

Zach chuckled, though he kept to himself his thoughts upon the subject of his host's juvenile outbursts. "Is there any possibility of a repetition of last night's display of temper? Should I intervene, do you think?"

The butler's aged face turned white with shock. "Certainly not, sir! His lordship would succumb to an apoplexy. Why, he would—"

"Your pardon, Peasby. I spoke in jest. Believe me, I would not think of interrupting. Not unless some large piece of furniture should smash against the door."

Realizing that the gentleman was teasing him, the servant smiled. "I will bring you a fresh pot of coffee, sir.

And when next I see Miss Preston, I will be happy to convey the information that you were looking for her."

Zach absently agreed to the fresh coffee, though his thoughts were on Judith and Lord Gillmore. What on earth could those two have to discuss? Nothing Judith would like, Zach would be bound. Deciding that he should stay close at hand, in case she had need of him, he told the butler he was going out into the garden. "Please inform the lady the minute she leaves the bookroom that I wish to speak with her."

"I shall tell her, sir."

Peasby was as good as his word, though it needed quick footwork on the old servant's part to catch up with Judith before she stormed out of the house. "In a rare taking, she was," he told Charles, the footman, when he chanced to encounter that strapping fellow in the servants' hall a few moments later. "Never seen the miss in such high color. Looked as if she might explode at any minute."

"Gor blimey," Charles replied. "Can't say as I blame her. Anyone would want to explode after a closed session with his vinegarship."

"Mind your tongue!"

The footman begged pardon and made himself scarce, but as he hurried away, the old butler chuckled. "His vinegarship," he repeated.

Judith ran from the house, speeding down the flagstone path to the little rustic garden. More angry than she could ever remembering being, she saw nothing of the delicate white blossoms of the pear trees, nor of the pink and lavender thrift that blanketed the surrounding area. She saw only the two wrought-iron benches and the man who waited for her there.

Dressed in a well-cut coat of Spanish blue superfine, with gray pantaloons that complimented the dark blue of the coat, he sat with his long legs wide apart, his elbows resting on his knees. In his hands he held a pear blossom that had fallen to the ground, turning it idly, yet not really seeing it. Judith did not question why she hurried toward him, she knew only that she wanted to tell him what had happened.

When Zach spotted her, the skirts of her primrose yellow muslin billowing out behind her as she ran, he tossed the flower aside and went to meet her. "You are upset," he said, taking both her hands in his and leading her toward the bench.

"No, sir, I am not upset. I am livid!"

"I stand corrected, ma'am."

They seated themselves upon the bench, their hands still entwined, and only after she took a deep breath and exhaled did he ask her about her visit with Lord Gillmore. "You need not tell me that it was unpleasant. The outrage smoldering in those big blue eyes reveals all I need to know upon that score. You may, however, wish to provide me with a detail or two so that I might know what we are up against."

"What we are up against?" Judith laughed, though the sound had little resemblance to her usual light, infectious gaiety. "You have hit upon the very crux of the conversation, sir. What we are up against—or rather what his lordship wishes us up against—is each other."

"I beg your pardon?"

"Lord Gillmore has grown weary of your interference with his heir. He wishes you distracted so that he may have a private moment with your brother. And I . . . I am to be that distraction. At least," she hurried to inform him, "that is his lordship's plan."

Unable to sit still, she pulled her hands from his, rose from the bench, then began to walk toward the far side of the garden. "He had the effrontery," she said, once Zach caught up with her, "to suggest that I do whatever was necessary to keep you away from the house. *Whatever was necessary!* As though my reputation, not to mention my honor, was of little consequence compared to his wishes.

"Then," she added, her breathing ragged with the re-membered anger, "he said it was a pity that I was such a peculiar-looking thing, for if I were handsomer, I would not need to resort to more than a little flattery and a flutter or two of my eyelashes."

To Judith's surprise, when she looked up at Zach, he was having a difficult time keeping a straight face. His gray eyes were alight with merriment, and his lips twitched at the corners. "And which," he asked, "angered you the most? The old goat's suggestion that you so demean your-self as to try to capture my interest, or his remarks upon your looks?"

Judith did not answer. She could not. Not with Zach smiling down at her as though he found her charming in the extreme. Not that he did, of course! He was merely amused, and that look he gave her—a look that went di-rectly to her midsection, causing it to feel as though a hun-dred butterflies had somehow taken up residence inside her—was but a trick of the morning sunlight.

"Little fawn," he said, softly. "That old martinet would not know a rare diamond if it fell from the sky and hit him solidly upon the head."

At his softly spoken words, those butterflies inside Ju-dith's stomach began to dance a reel.

"As for his lordship's suggestion that you distract me, I find that a capital notion."

"You . . . you do?"

"Of a certainty. I have been wondering this hour and more what excuse I might employ to get you to go for another walk with me. I cannot think you would wish to ride, but a walk might do you good."

"It would do me a world of good," she answered enthusiastically. "I have been champing at the proverbial bit these past few days. And though the Wimmers were wonderful to me—treating me as an honored guest, and not like the nuisance I must have been—you cannot know how happy I am to have put my invalidism behind me. Unfortunately," she said, sighing, "I dare not go in the lane, for I fled the house without a bonnet, and I cannot traverse rough terrain, for I am wearing slippers."

When she lifted the hem of her frock, he looked at the yellow kid slippers she was so obliging as to show him. "Walking to the weir is quite inadvisable," he said, "but is there some other direction we might take? Some route that is not too demanding?"

Judith pondered the question a moment, then she pointed toward a winding sheep's path that ran at a right angle to the route to the weir—a path cut into the land by generations of cloven hooves. "Down that way."

She allowed him to take her elbow, and as they followed the path that rose and fell with the rolling terrain, she told him more of her meeting in the bookroom. "His lordship said—" She stopped suddenly, her mouth open and her eyes wide with disbelief.

"Sir! Look at us. We have played right into Lord Gillmore's hands. Done exactly what he wanted. We have left the lieutenant alone, and now he will he hunted down, brought to ground, then forced to listen to his lordship's ultimatum about marrying my sister."

Zach shook his head. "He will not. Not unless the hunter sends his minions over to Rainsford Manor, for my brother has been there since early morning. He accepted Sir Thomas's invitation to try his luck at their trout stream."

"He is fishing?"

"Since daybreak. And unless I miss my guess, he is not likely to return until this evening."

For the first time since he had left her at Wimmer Cottage, Zach was treated to one of Judith's smiles. It was a sincere smile, wide and bright, and delivered in a manner guaranteed to make any gentleman feel himself fortunate to be with such a lady, walking in an idyllic setting of green countryside dotted with distant clusters of white sheep. Add to that a gentle May breeze at one's back, plus the soft, sweet scent of clover, and a man could not ask for more.

"That puts me in mind of something I had meant to ask you, ma'am."

"What?" she asked, the smile still in evidence. "If I like fishing?"

"No, that was not it," he said. "But do you? Like fishing, I mean."

"I cannot really say, for I have given it only one try. And that when I was about eleven years old. We were touring the Cotswolds that summer, and during a stop at the home of one of my stepfather's old school chums, the gentleman invited Papa Albert to fish his trout stream."

"Trout? But that is fly fishing. Surely your stepfather knew better than to take a child fly fishing."

"I have no doubt of it. However, Lilia and I thought it sounded great fun, and we gave poor Papa Albert no peace until he agreed to let us accompany him."

"I see," Zach said, "and was it great fun?"

"Ugh! What I remember most of the experience was standing in the brook, the water so cold my feet grew numb, and being admonished repeatedly to *shush*. Not that that was the worst of it."

Zach managed somehow to keep a straight face. "What could be worse than icy feet and enforced silence?"

"Fish!" she said with a shudder.

When Zach was obliged to cough to cover the laughter he could no longer contain, she lifted her chin haughtily, giving him a censuring look. "I might have known a man would not understand."

Trying for a serious demeanor, he said, "Then explain it to me, ma'am, so that I comprehend the whole."

After a moment's doubtful consideration, she finally continued. "Fish are such pretty creatures while swimming in the water, but if a person is so unfortunate as to catch one of the beasts, she soon discovers that they are not nearly so pretty out of their element."

"Not?"

"No, sir. They are all scaly, and their eyes bulge. And if a person manages to remove the barb and toss the vile-smelling creature upon the shore, it jumps about and twitches until the person vows she will never eat another morsel as long as she lives."

"And does the . . . er, *fisherperson* cry?"

"I did not, but Lilia—" She stopped abruptly, placing her hands on her hips as if she meant to argue. "Sir, you are making sport of me again."

"Only just a little," Zach said. "Pray forgive me, and do continue your story, for I find myself fascinated to hear the end of it. What happened after you tossed your prize onto the land?"

Judith was tempted to give him the snub he deserved, but owing to the contrite look in his eyes—a trick perfected over the years, no doubt, with other gullible women—she relented. "Lilia had remained on the shore, and as ill-luck would have it, the fish chanced to flap against the side of her boot. When that happened, she began to scream, setting up such a ruckus that Papa Albert was obliged to quit the brook and go see what he could do to quiet her."

Zach had another fit of coughing. "Then what did the beleaguered man do?"

"Lilia would not be calmed until Papa Albert had freed every trout caught that day. After being obliged to dump the entire contents of his creel back into the brook, he vowed before Heaven never again to take either Lilia or me any place."

"And did he abide by his vow?"

"Pshaw! Papa Albert had the sunniest disposition of any man I ever knew, and it was against his nature to remain angry for more than two minutes at a stretch. Furthermore, he delighted in the company of his family. A rather plebeian concept, I know, and not at all the thing for a true gentleman, but there it is."

All desire to laugh vanished, and Zach said quietly, "You were a very lucky little girl."

"Yes," she answered, equally quietly, "I was. But what of you? Your stepfather was cousin to mine. Was he much like Papa Albert?"

Zach did not answer her right away, and from the look upon his face, his thoughts were anything but happy. "It would appear, ma'am, that in the Gillmore family, amiability skips a generation. My brother is much like your Papa Albert. Andrew's father—my stepfather—was not."

They walked in silence for some time, the only sound the soft *trit, trit* of a meadow pipit startled as it hunted for food. Disliking the intrusion of the humans, the shy bird took wing, rising straight into the air, its soft, musical song audible until the little fellow was out of sight.

Shortly after the pipit's flight, Zach took Judith's hand

and tucked it into the crook of his arm. At his warm touch, Judith was almost as surprised as the little bird, though she did not flee. Foolish, of course, to turn giddy over such an unexceptional gallantry, but the nearness of him, and the feel of his rock-hard arm beneath her hand, turned her knees to India rubber.

Not wishing to betray the intensity of her reaction, she said the first thing that came into her head. "You said you wished to ask me something, sir. Something that had nothing whatever to do with fishing."

"Very true. I wanted to ask your opinion of Sir Thomas Rainsford."

Judith could not keep the surprise from her voice. "Sir Thomas? I scarcely know the man. Why do you ask?"

"I think the subject important. Will you indulge me by answering the question?"

Discerning that he was in earnest, she tried to be as honest as possible. "Sir Thomas seems a worthy enough person. Honorable as well as congenial. He is a bit ambitious to elevate his social position—a circumstance which sets up Lord Gillmore's hackles—but aside from the man's lamentable taste in clothes, I can find nothing to dislike in him."

"What would you think of him as a father-in-law for Miss Lilia?"

"For Lilia? Wherever did you get such a ridiculous notion? My sister does not even . . ." One look into those gray eyes, and she knew he was serious. "What have you heard, Zach? Has their been gossip of some kind about my sister?"

"Gossip? No. It is the testimony of my own eyes that convinces me your sister and Rainsford have formed an attachment for one another."

"Impossible. Believe me, you have misjudged the situation. I know my own sister. Lilia is very young, and completely without guile, so if she had developed a *tendre* for someone—Stan Rainsford or any other—she would have told me of it herself."

"Then I stand corrected, ma'am. Far be it from me to plant the seeds of doubt between siblings."

The words sounded sincere enough, but from the satirical way he raised that one eyebrow, Judith knew he believed his own appraisal of the situation and was only giving her time to adjust her assessment of her sister. Silently he waited, allowing her to come to her own conclusions as to whether or not Lilia might, indeed, have a secret or two she had not divulged.

"You say you saw something that made you think—"

"Both saw and heard."

Judith took a deep breath then exhaled slowly. "Tell me, sir."

"It was the afternoon you were taken to Wimmer Cottage. While the apothecary was abovestairs, completing his examination, Miss Lilia and young Rainsford were alone in the front parlor. She was crying and he was attempting to comfort her. They were deep in private conversation, and though it was never my intention to do so, I chanced to overhear what passed between them."

"Stan was comforting Lilia? How?"

"By allowing her to cry upon his shoulder."

Judith was silent for quite some time. Finally, she said, "Please continue."

"Under normal circumstances, I should have felt myself obliged to keep silent upon the subject under discussion, having been an unwilling auditor to a private conversation; however, when an elopement was mentioned, I thought it wisest to—"

"Elopement!" Judith felt as though she had been dealt a blow, one that left her dazed. "Surely you have misunderstood what you heard. Lilia and Mr. Rainsford barely know one another."

The look on Zach's face told her otherwise.

"From what I overheard, it is my belief that the two are convinced Miss Lilia will be forced to marry my brother. And it is this conviction that has prompted them to contemplate such a rash action."

Judith put her hand to her throat in hopes of silencing the accusations that rushed to escape, but anger won out over discretion. "I lay the blame for this entirely at Lord Gillmore's door," she said. "His lordship's edicts have precipitated this imprudent notion in my sister."

"Well," Zach drawled, "the old gentleman's foolishness may have triggered the idea of an elopement, but I suspect the two young people had already discussed the possibility of a future together."

"But that cannot be, for we barely know the Rainsfords."

"I should rather say, my girl that *you* barely know the Rainsfords. It is my belief that Miss Lilia is a frequent visitor to your neighbors."

From the serious tone in Zach's voice, Judith could not doubt that he had judged the situation correctly, yet she needed time to assimilate all he had told her. *An elopement.* How could Lilia be so lost to the scandal such an indiscretion would cause?

Judith thanked Heaven that Zach had overheard the conversation between Lilia and Stan, and she was grateful that he had seen fit to relay the startling information. Otherwise, she would have been unprepared to intervene before her sister committed an act guaranteed to ruin her completely. Nevertheless, at the moment she could not think what was best to do.

When she continued to walk, Zach fell in beside her. After a time, she said, "I cannot think Sir Thomas would like the match. And without his support, the young couple would have no means of livelihood."

"You are right about Sir Thomas. According to young Rainsford, his father fancies some great heiress for his daughter-in-law."

Judith snorted most inelegantly. "Mere pipe dreams. Though their estate is quite prosperous, and I believe Sir Thomas's wife was connected in some way to a noble house, to hope for an alliance with a great heiress is aiming a bit high. Of course, any father might reasonably expect his son's future wife to bring a respectable dowry to the marriage. Unhappily, Lilia cannot do so. Her sole contribution to the union would be her beauty and her sweetness of disposition."

Zach refrained from commenting upon a subject as private as a young lady's dowry, or lack there of. Instead, he said, "Do I understand, then, that you have no objections to the Rainsfords?"

"None at all. It goes without saying that I object to Lilia's plans for an elopement, but I do not suffer from Sir Thomas's delusions of grand alliances. My one reservation concerns my sister's financial security. I cannot like the idea of her aligning herself with a young man whose dependence rests solely upon the generosity of an angry father. Especially since it is a situation with which we are all too familiar."

She laughed, though the sound had little humor in it. "I would love to see Lord Gillmore's face if he should discover that Sir Thomas Rainsford—a man he refers to as 'That mushroom'—considers his lordship's granddaughter not good enough to marry his son."

Zach did not relate to Judith what he had overheard about an inheritance due the young man upon reaching his majority. It was his duty as a gentleman to tell someone in

Miss Lilia's family about the planned elopement, not to do so would have been unconscionable, but to divulge the whole of the conversation was to sink to the status of a gossip.

Besides, Zach had learned all he needed to know. Judith did not object to the Rainsfords, and that being true, he could now do whatever he wanted to assist the young couple.

Nine

The kissing gate! Had they come that far?

Judith had become preoccupied, pondering the fate of her lovely sister, and now she realized that she and Zach had walked at least two miles. They had been silent miles, for neither she nor Zach had spoken for quite some time. They might have continued walking forever had it not been for the kissing gate that blocked the sheep path.

An odd creation, the tall structure was designed to allow humans to pass through to the next estate, while keeping the bovine population within the confines of their owner's property. The gate consisted of a center pole, enclosed on three sides by a closely laid slat fence. Protruding from the pole at right angles were two dozen spindles that needed to be properly aligned before they could be rotated. Because of the protection from view offered by the three-sided fence, lovers were known to take advantage of the privacy offered therein to steal a kiss or two.

Giving little thought to the significance of the structure, Judith hurriedly apologized to Zach for having been inattentive. "Pray forgive me, sir, for my prolonged silence. I assure you, I had no wish to be rude."

"I did not perceive any rudeness. As a matter of fact, I was lost in thought."

"I cannot allow it to be true. I think you are just saying that to be kind."

"Oh?" He lifted one eyebrow. "Does that mean you think me incapable of thought?"

"No, no. I meant nothing of the kind, it is just—"

"It may surprise you to know, madam, that there are those who consider me a rather downy fellow."

Thinking she had insulted him again, she was all set to apologize a second time when she noticed the teasing light in his eyes.

"Downy?" she said sweetly, her own eyes wide in mock innocence. "Do you mean like a duck?"

After his initial shock, Zach had trouble schooling his lips into a serious pose. "Minx," he said.

Judith ignored the remark. "I own I find it extraordinary that a gentleman's friends should refer to him as a duck. Nonetheless, since you have on several occasions called me by some forest creature's name, I collect it is one of those London crazes. And for that reason, I have resolved to think nothing more of it."

Though the corners of his lips twitched, Zach wagged his finger at her in warning. "Have a care, madam."

"Truth to tell, sir, I would have thought *stallion* or *stag* more fitting appellations for a man of your size, but if duck is what you like, who am I to cavil."

He took a step toward her, and Judith had, perforce, to move back. "I warned you," he said.

When he advanced even closer, she chuckled and retreated another step. "I am not afraid of you, sir."

The words were no sooner out of her mouth than she felt something jab her between her shoulder blades. It was one of the gate spindles.

"You should be afraid," he said, a look of pure devilment

in those usually cool gray eyes, "for you have backed yourself into a very interesting corner."

Slowly he stretched his right arm out, resting his palm
against the fence, just beside her left shoulder. Then he
stretched out his other arm, placing that palm on the fence
mere inches from her right shoulder. Effectively imprison-
ing her, he bent his elbows and brought his head very close
to hers, whispering in her ear, "Are you frightened yet?"

At the feel of his warm breath upon her skin, Judith's
heart pounded painfully in her chest, but the reaction had
nothing whatever to do with fear. Nor did fear play any
part in those little pulses of excitement that inched their
way up and down her backbone when he nuzzled his chin
against her forehead.

"I could take you in there," he said, "inside the kissing
gate, and exact retribution upon you for making sport of
me."

"Retribution?" she asked rather breathlessly.

He stared at her lips while she said the word, his gaze
lingering long after the sound had faded into eternity.

"First," he said, "to show you what a dangerous fellow
I am, I might nibble at your lovely throat, just there, beneath the lace of your fichu."

His gaze traveled to the side of her neck, and Judith's
skin grew so warm she thought surely he had touched her
with more than his eyes.

"Then," he said, "I would work my way round to that
spot just behind your ear—that spot where the flesh is delicate and sensitive, and where those little curls come loose
from your coiffure."

"Wh-what would you do next?" she asked.

"I might pull the pins from your hair and comb my fingers through the thick silk. Then, once the tresses were

loose and free, I would bury my face in them, breathing deeply of their sweet perfume."

A sigh escaped Judith's lips. So mesmerized was she by his imaginative description that she was tempted to shake her head to see if the hair might actually have come loose.

"After I had memorized the texture and aroma of your hair," he murmured softly, "I would then make a pilgrimage—a sort of voyage of discovery—placing unhurried, exploratory kisses upon the enticing curve of your jaw. Upon your eyelids. Upon the tip of that enchanting little nose."

Judith was having difficulty breathing, and for the first time, she knew fear—fear that she might faint from anticipation before Zach even began his exploration. Nervously she licked her lips, and the action brought his attention back to her mouth.

"Finally," he whispered, his voice noticeably husky, "I would kiss your mouth. I would cover your lips with my own. Warming them. Tasting them. Teasing them until you were unable to stop yourself from slipping your arms around my neck and kissing me back."

Having given her fair warning of what would befall her, Zach leaned forward again and began the assault he had described. Gently he brushed aside the edge of the fichu, tracing his warm lips along that spot on her neck.

At his touch, Judith's knees threatened to give way beneath her, and to keep from falling, she caught hold of the lapels of his coat. "Zach," she said, the word so breathy she was not certain she had actually spoken it. "Zach, I—"

"Beg pardon, Your Honor," a boy's voice said, "but I got to fetch that lamb."

After a quickly muttered oath, Zach pulled Judith's head against his chest, then he squared his shoulders, using their breadth to shield her from the young shepherd's sight.

Looking over his right shoulder, Zach spied a small pink-nosed ball of wool standing just a few feet from the gate, its spindly legs shaking with fear and exhaustion. The lamb had wandered too far from its dam, and now it bleated its high-pitched *baa baa* as though its heart might break.

He motioned for the shepherd to come get the animal. "Do what you must, lad."

While he spoke, Judith scrunched her eyes tightly shut, as though her not being able to see the boy would keep him from seeing her. And as she stood thus, letting Zach shield her from view, she was uncertain what feeling was uppermost inside her. Was it embarrassment at being caught at the kissing gate like some village lightskirt? Or was it disappointment at being deprived of her kiss once again?

She had not yet sorted out her thoughts when the boy retrieved the little lamb, set it around his neck like a snowy fleeced scarf, and hurried back down the path toward the remainder of the fold. Whatever the outcome of her quandary—embarrassment or disappointment—it was clear to Judith that she was destined never to know the thrill of Zach's promised assault.

"Come," he said when the lad was out of sight. "I will take you home."

From the calmness of his voice, it was obvious that Zach experienced none of the confusion that plagued Judith—confusion that left her emotions raw and her mind befuddled. Since there was nothing to be done but acquiesce to his suggestion, she turned and began walking rather hurriedly in the direction from whence they had come.

After a time, wishing to break the uncomfortable silence that loomed between them, she thanked Zach for the gifts he had sent while she was at Wimmer Cottage. "You may be interested to know, sir, that even though Master Jeremy Wimmer was at first unable to open the secret box you sent him, after many hours of investigation, he finally solved the mystery. I do not have to tell you of his delight when he found the bright new shilling hidden inside."

The remainder of their walk was accomplished in innocuous chit chat, and only when they reached the garden at Gillmore House was Judith able to look Zach in the face. "Thank you," she said, "for the outing. I shall leave you now, for I feel certain that my mother will be wondering what has become of me."

After making her a formal bow, Zach said, "Of course, madam."

Picking up the hem of her primrose muslin, Judith all but ran across the garden.

Zach watched her the entire time, as she approached the house then opened a heavy wooden door at the rear. Even after she disappeared from view, he stood thus for several minutes, observing the spot where he had last seen her, all the while cautioning himself to remember his reason for coming to Gillmore House. That reason had nothing to do with willowy nymphs, or with eyes as clear and blue as a morning sky, or with lips so soft they begged to be kissed.

After a time, he turned and walked to the stables. Once the gelding was saddled, Zach let the horse choose his own pace down the carriageway, allowing him to gallop off his freshness. When they reached the lane, however, Zach took control, turning the animal toward Rainsford Manor. His decision made, he meant to have a talk with a certain young man whose hopes for the future needed a bit of assistance.

"You are an idiot!" Judith muttered for at least the hundredth time. "A fool. A simpleton."

Seeking some solitude in which to compose her thoughts after what had nearly happened at the kissing gate, she went directly to the picture gallery, rather than to the bed-chamber she shared with her sister. But after closing the door behind her and turning the heavy brass key in the lock to insure her privacy, she still could not think clearly. Unable to sit quietly, she traversed the length of the gallery several times, muttering to herself as she walked.

"You are the veryest looby," she said, "if you think that little episode at the kissing gate held any significance for Zachery Camden. He is a man of the world, and it is not to be marveled at that he would indulge in a bit of flirtation to beguile the time while he waits to return to town. Depend upon it, the encounter meant nothing to him.

"Less than nothing!"

The problem was, it had meant the world to Judith. In fact, she was very much afraid she was falling in love with the man.

"Foolish, foolish woman!"

She stopped beside Lilia's favorite chair, and while resting one knee on the uncushioned seat, she gazed beyond the ornately carved wooden back and through the diamond-paned window to the stretch of green park below. The tranquil scene had no beneficial effect upon her. Her senses in a turmoil, she quit the chair and began to pace again.

How had this happened? How had she come to love a man she had known for a mere six days? Moreover, a man whose very lifestyle was repugnant to her. A gambler!

Never mind that he had been kindness itself to her after her injury on the horse. Never mind that he had behaved in a most gentlemanly manner when with the Wimmers, always treating them with the utmost respect, not once acting as though they were not his social equal. And never mind that he had stood up to Lord Gillmore on more than one occasion.

He was still a gambler. The very antithesis of the steady,

reliable man who figured in all her dreams of love and marriage.

Marriage?

Judith had certainly rushed that fence, for Zachery Camden had expressed by neither word nor deed the least desire to share anything more with her than a few kisses.

She sighed, remembering those moments at the kissing gate, moments in which her skin had positively vibrated with awareness at his closeness. She recalled the way her pulse had raced at his smile. How she had waited, her breathing suspended, for him to take her in his arms and kiss her.

Worst of all, Judith realized it was not just Zach's kisses she wanted. She wanted to be near him. Almost from the first day she had met him, she had spent those intervals between their meetings waiting for the next encounter. In his presence she came alive. When with him she felt, somehow, as if she had come home. As if she had finally met the most important person of her lifetime. Her friend. Her companion. Her lover.

While Judith paced in the picture gallery at Gillmore House, mediating the argument that raged between her heart and her inner voice, Zach galloped past Sir Thomas's pretentious brick manor house and turned his horse toward the Rainsford stables, all the while bandying a few heated words with his own conscience. Unfortunately, the outcome of his debate was no more fruitful than Judith's had been, and it ended with only one solid decision. He vowed never again to be alone with Judith Preston.

"If you cannot keep your hands off her, than keep your distance!"

Zach had come to Dorset to act as a buffer between his

brother and any plans concocted to compromise the lad into matrimony. Despite that fact, and his own long-held resolve never to become a tenant for life, Zach had come very close this morning to compromising as fine a young woman as he had ever met.

Fine? What a flavorless word for so delicious a creature. Judith Preston was the most entrancing female Zach had ever met—lively, energetic, and filled with a joy for life. She was also the most genuine and the most loyal woman he had ever known.

The majority of Zach's distaff acquaintances, his mother included, spared little thought for the happiness of their families. They were interested only in wealth, position, and all the things money could buy.

Of course, Judith was interested in money as well—she made no secret of the fact—but her wishes had nothing to do with a desire to purchase luxuries and jewels to impress her acquaintances. Her concern was for the security money would provide for the people she loved.

Lost in thoughts of Judith and the way her blue eyes had shone when he had bent to kiss her, not to mention that bewitching way her lips had quivered, as if waiting for his touch, he almost allowed the gelding to trot past the stable.

"Damnation!" he muttered, though his annoyance had little to do with either the horse or the stable.

Zach was very much afraid that his vexation had more to do with a certain gamine-faced enchantress, for he had just realized that if he honored his vow and kept his distance from her, he would never know the feel of her lips beneath his. Never experience the heady sensation of gathering her slender body in his arms and pressing her close against his heart. Never discover those little special ways to delight her and—

"Afternoon, sir," one of the young grooms said, doffing his cap politely.

The greeting brought Zach's thoughts back to the business at hand, and he reined in the horse, nodding to the lad who stood in the doorway, a strong aroma of horse and hay about his person.

"Be ye wishful of returning the gelding, sir? Is summit wrong?"

"Not at all," Zach replied, leaning forward and patting the animal's glossy black neck. "He is an excellent fellow. Intelligent, quick, and responsive."

The lad smiled. "I'm that glad to hear it, sir. But if ye b'aint come to return the horse, be there ought I can do for ye?"

"You may direct me to Mr. Stanbury Rainsford."

The lad pointed a none-too-clean finger to an area some distance from the stables. "Mr. Stan be in the paddock, exercising Bess. Ye want I should show you, sir?"

Zach shook his head, then he fetched a shilling from his vest pocket and tossed the coin to the groom. "I shall not keep you from your work."

Catching the silver in mid-air, the lad smiled then disappeared into the dimness of the stable. Meanwhile, Zach urged the gelding around to the exercise yard where he found Stan Rainsford astride Bess, the beautiful roan filly.

Stan was putting the three-year-old through her paces. And very fast paces they were. In fact, Zach doubted he had ever seen so young a horse with that much finesse.

"She is a marvelous animal," he said several minutes later when Stan gave the filly into a groom's care then walked over to the rail fence that divided the paddock from the carriageway. "As fine a filly as I have ever seen."

The slender young man beamed with pride. Running his fingers through his damp, sunny blond hair, he said, "Bess is descended from Godolphin Barb. And if the last few days' runs are anything to judge by, she may soon prove to be even faster than Eclipse."

Zach was accustomed to such comparisons. Every likely equine he had ever heard touted was compared to Eclipse, racing's only undefeated horse. In this instance, however, he suspected the remark just might be true.

"If you have a few moments to spare, Rainsford, I have a proposition I think may interest you."

While Stan vaulted over the rail fence, Zach dismounted and tied the gelding's reins to the top rail. "Shall we walk a bit?"

Stan fell into step with him, waiting politely for Zach to begin the conversation. He had not long to wait, for Zach got right to the point.

"Several days ago, I overheard a conversation between you and Miss Lilia Gillmore. I need to know if what I heard is true."

Though Mr. Rainsford stiffened, all signs of his previous friendliness gone, Zach continued. "Are you wishful of marrying the young lady?"

"I cannot see, sir, where that is any concern of yours."

"You are right, of course. It is not. But if you will oblige me by answering the question truthfully, I promise you I shall make it worth your while."

The young man did not unbend; far from it, for his brown eyes flashed with undisguised resentment. "I am not a child to be bribed, sir. Nor do I wish to discuss Miss Gillmore with you or anyone else."

Zach took no offense at Mr. Rainsford's indignation, though he did advise him quite cordially not to be such a young stiff rump.

"If I remember correctly, lad, you told Miss Lilia you needed eight hundred pounds to enable you to enter Friday's race meet. I am prepared to give you that amount, if that is your wish, and I shall not renege even if you tell me you have no interest whatsoever in the young lady. However, I must know up front your intentions as they relate to her."

After a rather lengthy silence, Stan muttered something beneath his breath, then he said simply, "I love Lilia, and I have every intention of making her my wife. No matter what my father, or her grandfather, or even Lieutenant Gillmore say to the contrary, she and I will—"

"You may safely leave my brother out of all your reckoning. While anyone must find Miss Lilia a beautiful and charming young lady, you may believe me when I tell you that Andrew has no interest in settling down at this time."

Zach gave the lad a moment to assimilate this information, then he added, "What is between you and your father is something you must handle, and I shall say no more on that head. As for Lord Gillmore, he is not the chit's guardian, and no matter how he may rant and rave, he has no legal say in the matter of her marriage. Mrs. Dorothy Gillmore is the only person whose approval you must have."

Obviously much struck by this piece of news, Stan remained silent for some time. Finally he said, "You are serious, sir, about the money?"

"Quite serious."

It was obvious the young man had not yet learned to dissemble, for while the light of hope shone in his brown eyes, doubt and indecision were writ plainly upon his face. "Eight hundred pounds is a lot of money."

"True. And your point is?"

Stan gave him a challenging look. "Why would you be willing to risk such a large sum on me?"

At the forthright question, Zach chuckled. "Have you not heard? I am an inveterate gambler."

Ten

That evening the gentlemen remained at Rainsford Manor and did not return to Gillmore House until the ladies were all abed. Not that Judith was asleep when she heard the horses gallop up the carriageway. Far from it. As a result of the war being waged inside her, she had been unable to close her eyes, but upon hearing the brothers make their way up the stairs and to their rooms, she breathed a sigh and drifted off almost immediately into undisturbed sleep.

She was roused from her slumber not many hours later by the furtive entry of one of the young kitchen maids into her bedchamber. The day was quite new, with only a faint gray light showing at the window where the drapery was not completely closed, so Judith knew something important had happened. Though instantly awake, she said nothing, for the maid tiptoed stealthily across the faded carpet, her destination the small dressing room where Lilia slept.

"Miss," whispered the servant, tapping Lilia upon the shoulder. "Miss. It's Gemma. I have a note for you."

When Lilia did not waken, but mumbled something about not wanting any breakfast, the girl persisted. "Miss," she said, slightly louder. "Mr. Stan give me this note for you. He says he will wait for you in the garden."

"What?" Lilia's voice was thick with sleep, but she sounded awake. "Did you say that Stan is here?"

"Yes, miss. In the garden. He give me this note, along with a shilling for delivering the note to you personal like."

Judith heard the crinkle of paper, then moments later Lilia bid the maid close the connecting door so she could light the candle. Just before the door shut, she whispered, "While I read, Gemma, find me a frock I can slip into quickly."

In a surprisingly short time, the door opened again and both Lilia and the servant tiptoed past Judith's bed. Since she was obviously not to be the recipient of her sister's confidence, Judith feigned sleep. As soon as the two conspirators quit the chamber, however, she threw back the covers and ran to the clothespress, removing the first dress she put her hands to and hastily donning it.

Fearing that Stan might have brought a carriage so that he and Lilia could elope that very morning, Judith did not waste time pinning up her hair; instead, she tossed the loose braid back over her shoulder, thrust her bare feet into a pair of boots, then hurried from the room. She knew she had no time to lose if she was to stop them from following this ruinous course, yet she forced herself to move stealthily, lest she wake anyone else in the house.

Not wanting to pass the kitchen where she might be seen by the servants busy with the preparation of the morning meal, Judith chose to go out the front entrance. After working the thick iron bolt loose, she opened the wooden door a matter of inches, then slipped outside, closing the door behind her.

Though a few patches of fog still clung to the low lying areas in the park, the sun had drawn dusky pink streaks across the gray-blue sky, and Judith could see well enough to run without stumbling. When she reached the flagstone path, she slowed her pace to a walk, continuing down the gently sloping hill until she spied her sister, who stood inside the circle of Stan Rainsford's arms, her face buried in the hollow of his shoulder.

The couple were too involved with one another to notice Judith, so she was able to conceal herself behind a clump of overgrown hawthorn bushes that grew at the corner of the garden. Kneeling in the dew-soaked grass, she ignored the moisture that quickly permeated her muslin skirt, concerned only with discovering the true purpose for this clandestine meeting, and hoping she would not be forced to rush forward and physically restrain her sister from leaving the premises.

Praying as well that she would not be obliged to reveal herself for the eavesdropper she was, she listened in upon the private conversation.

"I cannot credit my ears," Lilia said, lifting her head from the young man's shoulder. Her voice had a watery quality, as if she had been crying, though there was wonder in her tone. "You have the entire eight hundred pounds?"

"The full amount, my love."

Removing a handkerchief from inside his coat, Stan dabbed gently at her damp cheeks. "I know I should not have come to you like this, but I could wait no longer to acquaint you with the happy news."

"The news is most certainly happy, but how is it possible? Yesterday you said we must abandon all our dreams for the future. At that time, you had given up hope of ever getting the money."

"True. But that was before Mr. Camden came to see me."

"Mr. Camden? What has he to do with us?"

"Everything. I have the eight hundred from him."

No! Judith clamped her hand over her mouth to keep from crying out. Zach could not have given Stan money for an elopement. She could not—would not—believe such a despicable act of him. True, he wanted to protect his brother from an unwanted marriage, but not at the expense of an innocent girl's reputation. He was incapable of such treachery.

"And what of the jockey?" Lilia asked. "Is he still available, do you think?"

Jockey? Was her sister bereft of her senses? An eloping pair would need to hire a chaise and a coachman, but certainly not a jockey.

"As soon as I had Mr. Camden's draft in my hand, I sent one of the grooms to fetch Joseph Harvey. He should be here in plenty of time for the race."

Race? Jockey? Had Judith gone mad or had they?

"I will be quite busy in the next three days," Stan said, "so do not be concerned if you do not see me in that time."

"No, no," Lilia replied. "I shall miss you, of course, but I shall be content knowing that you are doing what is necessary to secure our future."

Judith exhaled noisily. Stan would be busy for the next few days—busy securing their future. Whatever that might portend, of one thing Judith could be certain, an elopement was not imminent.

"I shall be obliged," Stan continued, "to walk Bess to the race track, so I have decided to take her there today. In that way, she will be rested by Friday when the heat takes place."

Lilia seemed distressed by this information, for she caught hold of Stan's sleeve. "But what of the blacklegs? I thought you told me those despicable fellows would stop at nothing to insure that the betting went their way. Might they not try to harm Bess?"

Stan covered her hand with his, his manner reassuring, though his face betrayed his concern. "I shall not leave Bess's side until time for the heat. Furthermore, there will be a groom with us at all times, a loaded pistol in his possession. If anyone should think to injure the filly, or try to put something in her hay to give her the colic, they will find us at the ready."

"Please," Lilia said, throwing her arms around Stan's neck, "be careful."

He returned her embrace with added fervor. "Have no fear, my love. You may trust that I will take every precaution."

After one final squeeze, he put her from him. "When next I see you, I shall have won the race and whatever prize money victory carries with it. The winner takes the entire purse, don't you know, a purse that often totals several thousand pounds. With that much money in my pocket, I shall be able to ask your mother for your hand."

"Oh, Stan. I shall say a prayer for us, and for Bess."

"Bless you, my angel."

Judith averted her gaze so she did not spy upon their final goodbye. Eavesdropping was despicable enough, she would not lower herself to the level of a Peeping Tom.

Their parting was briefer than Judith had anticipated, and within seconds she heard footfalls very close to the hawthorn bushes. Unable to flee, her only recourse was to make herself as small as possible. Since she was already on her knees, she tucked herself into a ball and hid her head beneath her arms.

Fortunately, when her sister passed by the hawthorns, the young lady was too concerned with her own thoughts even to glance at the bushes. Within a matter of seconds, Judith heard Stan hurry off in the opposite direction. Once they were both gone, she heaved a sigh of relief, though she remained where she was for a full minute just to be on the safe side.

"You may get up now," said a deep voice, startling her into a gasp.

Embarrassed at having been caught in a reprehensible act, not to mention in a most unladylike position, Judith scrambled to get up. Unfortunately, in her haste to find her feet, she stepped on the hem of her skirt and pitched forward. However, thanks to a strong arm that reached out and caught her round the waist then lifted her so that her back was flush with a rock-hard chest, she was spared another painful encounter with the ground.

"Unhand me!" she ordered, shaken by the contact with that manly chest. "How dare you!"

"How dare *I?*"

Zach chuckled, still holding her fast. "Madam, may I remind you that it was not *I* who was burrowed beneath a bush like a hedgehog, listening to a very private conversation."

Though the truth of his observation was unanswerable, Judith took exception to the unflattering likening of herself to a spiny hedgehog. "Must you be forever calling me by some animal's name?"

"Only when you put me in mind of one. For instance, I am reminded at the moment of a spitting cat. Or," he added, peering over her shoulder to view the front of her sodden and rather muddy skirt, "a creature of rather less fastidious habits."

Judith looked down at her filthy dress then felt herself blush. "I . . . I suppose I do appear rather a mess."

"Not at all," he corrected pleasantly, "merely unconventional."

Still holding her against him, his arm around her waist, Zach was less interested in the state of her dress than he was her undress, for she had seen fit to don her frock without the dubious benefit of her stays. More than a little intrigued by the feel of her slender body unbound by its usual restrictions, he made no effort to release her. Instead, he lifted her thick braid, placing it neatly across the front of her shoulder. "I like your hair," he said.

Judith's hands all but flew to her head, and she tried what she could to brush back the wispy tendrils that danced about her temple and her neck. "I . . . I was in such a hurry to get out here that I did not spare the time to do up my hair."

"Do not worry on my account," he said softly.

Giving in to an almost overwhelming desire to feel those wispy curls brush across his lips, he nuzzled his cheek against her temple. "I find nothing to dislike," he murmured, "in either your hair or your clothing."

Judith relaxed against him for a moment; then, as if she had just become conscious of her lack of underpinnings, she pushed at his arm. "Let me go," she said.

He did as she asked, of course, but not without a pang of regret. She fit so nicely in his arms that Zach was—

Damnation! It was less than twenty-four hours since he had vowed to keep his hands off her, and here he was, pawing her again. What was it about the woman that made him want to be near her all the time?

All the time? Where the deuce had that idea come from?

Wanting to touch a woman—wanting to hold her close and kiss her until she was breathless—that was one thing, but wanting to be with her all the time, that was something entirely different. Zach had no interest in being with one woman for life. He never had and he never would.

He definitely did not.

Positively did not.

Though if he did want such a thing, Judith would be the very lady who—

No!

Not wanting to pursue that line of thought, he asked

rather sharply, "Did you hear all you wished to know while you were playing hedgehog?"

At his accusatory question, her face turned rose red. "It was not what you think."

"Was it not? Then might one inquire why you deemed it necessary to conceal your presence from your sister and young Rainsford?"

On the defensive, she countered with, "Might one inquire why you bet eight hundred pounds on Stan's horse?"

"I did not bet—"

"Do not try to deny it. That is why Stan came here so early, to tell Lilia that he would be at the race course for the next three days."

"And he told her that I had made a wager on his horse?"

"Not in those words, but—"

"I thought not."

Judith looked up at him, disillusionment pulling the corners of her pretty mouth downward. "Why did you do it?" she asked quietly.

Zach's reply was equally quiet. "I did it because I wanted to. I thought it would help the lad. Enable him to—"

"How can it help anyone to risk such a large sum of money?"

"Eight hundred? I assure you, I can afford it."

"But what if the horse loses? What will you do then? Will you compound the mistake by betting double or nothing? Very few people can afford to lose sixteen hundred pounds. But even if they could, it would be an iniquity, for that much money would support a prudent person for years. Perhaps two people!"

"I hope it may," he said.

Her anger revived by his reply, she said, "Gamblers! They are always so glib. Always ready with an answer for every argument."

Before he could defend himself against the accusation, she turned and ran toward the house, her skirts flying, and as Zach watched her, he was amazed anew by her speed and her graceful, athletic gait.

He caught up with her just as she reached the front door, seizing her wrist to detain her so he could explain. When she turned and looked up at him, however, her blue eyes were wide with sadness, and he forgot everything but the overpowering need he felt to take her in his arms and comfort her.

Apparently, Judith had other ideas. She stared coldly at his fingers wrapped around her wrist, until he released his grasp; then once she was free, she backed away.

Zach allowed her to retreat, convinced that she wanted to hear nothing more from him at that moment. "Please," he said, "do not worry. I am confident that all will come out well."

"I hope you may be right," she said, her tone anything but optimistic.

Without another word, she pushed open the heavy front door, entered the house, then closed the door behind her.

When Judith reached her bedchamber, she found Lilia tucked up in her bed in the dressing room, feigning sleep. Deciding it was time she had a talk with that secretive damsel, but certain her position would be stronger if she were not wearing the evidence of her eavesdropping, she removed the muddy dress and donned her linen wrapper.

Disposing herself upon the foot of her sister's bed, Judith chose not to dignify the charade of sleep by pretending to wake her. Instead, she said, "Why did you not tell me that you had developed a *tendre* for Stan Rainsford?"

Lilia sat up instantly, her lovely face wreathed in smiles,

"Best of sisters," she said, "please do not be angry with me. Not today. Not when I am the happiest, the most fortunate person in Dorset. No, I am the luckiest girl in the entire world!"

"I am pleased that you are happy, Lilia, but—"

"Can you believe it? By this time next week, I shall be betrothed to Stan, for he is to ask Mama for my hand directly the race meet is over."

The day was well advanced before Judith saw Zach again. She was coming from the corridor that led to the kitchen rooms, and he had just entered the front door. He must have been out riding, for his black hair was windblown, and his well-polished boots bore splatters of mud.

"Well met," he said, waiting for her at the bottom of the wide stone staircase, "for I have something that belongs to you. Something I wish to return."

Torn between her happiness at seeing him and her desire to disassociate herself from one who represented all she disliked, Judith's reply was far from friendly. "Something of mine? Truly, sir, I cannot imagine what that may be."

"Please," he said, motioning toward one of the little rosewood settees that flanked the hall fireplace. "I know you are vexed with me, but may we not sit down like two friends?"

Judith strode across the room, her body rigid, then she seated herself in the middle of the settee, her back ramrod straight. Though it was mean-spirited of her to dispose herself so that he was obliged to remain standing, she could not seem to help herself.

Zach did not appear to take offense at her churlishness, but merely reached inside his vest pocket and withdrew a delicate gold chain, an enameled heart suspended from it. "The stakes you gave me to hold when I first arrived," he said, presenting the trinket to her. "Since Miss Lilia has acknowledged her partiality for Stan Rainsford, our wager has, in effect, reached a stalemate."

When Judith did not immediately take the necklace from him, Zach set his hat and gloves upon the mantelpiece, then he carefully slipped the gold chain over her head, adjusting the heart so it was not lost inside her fichu. "There," he said, his hands lingering upon her shoulders, his warm thumbs resting on either side of the hollow of her throat. "Your keepsake is back where it belongs, around your lovely neck."

After touching the little heart, Judith looked up at him, her face warm with embarrassment. "I should never have made such a wager. It was wrong of me, especially when I hold gambling in such abhorrence."

Zach sighed; then, unable to stop himself, he took her face in his hands, looking deeply into her innocent eyes. "Do not fret, my sweet, for I cannot believe you so dissipated as to be past reclaiming."

"No?" she asked softly.

"I am sure of it. Besides, all of life is a gamble. To gain something of real value, each of us must be willing to risk that which makes us comfortable."

When she would have spoken, Zach bent and slowly brushed his lips against hers. The contact was fleeting, lasting for only a moment, but it sent shock waves through his body. Then, though he knew he should not, he kissed her again, allowing his mouth to linger upon her sweet lips just long enough to elicit a response from her.

"Zach," Judith whispered when he broke away, ending the kiss that had left her senses spinning and her soul yearning for more. "I—"

"Shh," he said, placing his fingertips against her mouth to still her words. "We will talk later. For now, just think about what I said."

Eleven

The entire company met for the evening meal, and though it had been more than a week since they had all dined together, their time apart had not noticeably improved the conviviality of the gathering. As before, Mrs. Gillmore and Andrew contributed most to the table conversation, with Zach and Judith answering only when spoken to. As for Lilia, that damsel sat quietly, a far-away, dreamy expression in her brown eyes.

Lord Gillmore consumed his dinner with scant notice of what he ate or what was being said around him. Caring little whether there was silence or incessant chatter, he spent the entire time staring at his heir, the smile upon his gaunt face reminiscent of an Egyptian crocodile contemplating his next victim. Finally, just as the ladies were about to withdraw, leaving the gentlemen to their port, he made his move, addressing Lieutenant Gillmore in a manner he felt certain would produce results favorable to his cause.

"Gillmore," he said, his tone a peculiar blend of conciliation and orders, "I have wished to speak privately with you for some time, but something or other always prevents it. Now, I believe, would be an excellent opportunity for us to talk."

Congratulating himself upon his quickness, his lordship

continued. "If you will join me in the bookroom, sir, I will
have Peasby bring you a glass of port in there. Meanwhile,
your brother may partake of his wine in the drawing room
with the ladies."

When he looked at his daughter-in-law, all conciliation
was gone. In this instance, it was obvious he expected to
be obeyed. "Dorothy, it would displease me to learn that
you and your daughters were remiss in keeping Mr. Camden entertained until such time as my heir and I have completed our discussion."

The order given, his lordship paid no further attention
to the females. Instead, he waited for some show of resis-
tance from one or other of the young men. He was almost
disappointed when Lieutenant Gillmore acquiesced without argument.

"I am at your disposal, my lord."

His lordship turned quickly to scowl at Zach, lest
opposition come from that quarter. His thick, iron-
gray eyebrows met above the bridge of his nose as if in
challenge, but the gauntlet was not picked up. Zach merely
smiled at him, then gave his attention to Dorothy Gillmore.

"Madam," he said, "if I do not intrude upon you and
your family, I would be pleased to join you for a cup of
tea. And if you should not dislike it, might I beg the favor
of a few selections on the pianoforte?"

Mrs. Gillmore looked from her father-in-law to Zachery
Camden, indecision not the least of the emotions showing
upon her face. "I . . . I should be pleased to have your company, sir, if that is your wish. As for the music, that would
be better left to my daughter's capable fingers."

The matter settled, Zach escorted Dorothy Gillmore to
the drawing room, followed closely by Judith and Lilia.
Within seconds, Lord Gillmore, leaning upon the arm of
one of his footmen, preceded his heir to the bookroom.

Once inside the private sanctum, his lordship settled himself in the comfortable, leather-covered chair behind the ornate walnut desk, bidding Andrew take the only other seat, a wooden contraption that when unfolded did double duty as a stepladder. After ordering the servant from the room, the old gentleman got immediately to the business at hand.

"You ain't leg shackled," he said, the statement a declaration not a question.

"No, sir," Andrew replied, "I am not married. Nor," he added, "have I any wish to be so. Not at this time. I have only just lately joined my regiment, and—"

"Do not be forever interrupting!" his lordship ordered, "for I have no wish to listen to the plans of a halfling still too inexperienced to know what is best for him."

Andrew bristled, but he kept his tongue between his teeth, choosing instead to let the old martinet have his say and be done with it.

"I have decided," Lord Gillmore said, "that you shall marry my granddaughter. Since I do not hold with long betrothals, the wedding will take place the week following the final reading of the banns. You may use the betrothal time to resign your commission and settle your affairs in town, sending any outstanding bills to my man of business. Once you and Lilia are wed, you will, of course, reside here at Gillmore House, where I can see to your instruction regarding those things required of a good landlord. I must have you for my heir—I can do nothing to change that fact—but by Heaven, I will see you whipped into shape before I put my spoon in the wall."

His lordship laid out his entire plan for his heir's future, then he settled back in his chair, a look of satisfaction upon his face. Only then did Andrew speak.

"Sir, I can appreciate your disappointment at having to

pass along all you hold dear to one you feel both unworthy of such an honor and unqualified to manage it. But, as you say, there is nothing you can do to change the fact. God willing, I will be the next Baron Gillmore.

"However," he added affably, "I cannot do as you ask."

His lordship glowered at his heir. "It was not a request. And you *will* do as I say."

"No, sir. I will not."

"Have a care, you young jackanapes. You forget the purse strings are still within my control."

"It is not so much that I forget, sir, as that I do not care."

"Balderdash. Such shabby genteel pretensions will not serve, Gillmore. I know that the pockets of young lieutenants are always to let."

"Not mine. It is none of your business, of course, but my brother is most generous with me, making me an allowance that more than satisfies my needs."

Obviously surprised by this piece of news, Lord Gillmore banged his cane against the side of the desk. "I wish to hear no more of this foolishness! You will do as I say, and there's an end to it."

Speaking slowly and precisely so there was no mistaking his meaning, Andrew said, "I will not resign my commission. I will not remove to Gillmore House. And I will not marry your granddaughter."

The words had only just left Andrew's mouth when the old gentleman set up an unconscionable din, abusing the desk with his cane. With each pounding of the stick, his face grew a brighter red, rage making the veins in his neck so engorged that Andrew feared he might at any moment fall into an apoplectic fit.

"You shall obey me!" he shouted.

"No," Andrew answered quietly. "Even if I entertained feelings for Miss Lilia, which I do not, I should not be persuaded to offer for her simply because you demand it. Besides," he added before his lordship could interrupt again, "my cousin Lilia is promised to another."

While the present and the future Barons Gillmore waged a battle of wills in the bookroom, the remainder of the party sat in the drawing room listening to Lilia perform upon the pianoforte. A talented young lady, her nimble fingers glided easily over the keys, and while the charming notes of Scarlatti's *Già il sole dal Gange* inspired Mrs. Gillmore and Zach to contemplate the glories of the sunset reflected in the Ganges River, Judith contemplated the gentleman's handsome profile. Especially his well-shaped lips.

All of life is a gamble.

Zach's words still echoed in Judith's ears, even though it had been several hours since he had spoken them. He had bid her think about what he said. But how could she do so, when all she wanted to remember was his kiss?

Such a soft, tender kiss—a mere touching of lips—yet it had toyed with her very soul, compelling her to admit something she would have done much better to keep hidden from herself: She loved Zachery Camden. Loved him completely. Irrevocably. And though she told herself it was folly to give her heart to such a man—to a gambler—the warning came too late.

Zach had said that all of life was a gamble, that to gain something of value, a person must be willing to risk that which makes them comfortable. Was she willing to risk whatever comfort life might offer her, and take a chance upon a gambler?

The answer was a resounding *yes!* If that man was Zachery Camden. Poverty, even privation, were well worth the risk if she could be with Zach, for she loved him and

longed to spend the rest of her life with him, happy to
chance her fate with his.

Not that he had asked such a commitment from her. Not
by word or deed. All he had done was kiss her, and though
that kiss had sealed Judith's fate, she had to face the fact
that it might not have been for Zach the life altering event
it was for her.

The joy of Scarlatti had given way to the magical beauty
of Mozart when Lilia's fingers abruptly ceased their movement across the keys. A racket was coming from the bookroom, and everyone in the drawing room gave the disturbance
their full attention. In addition to the loud and repeated banging that sounded suspiciously like the dismantling of furniture, there were also shouts.

"What!" Lord Gillmore yelled. "My granddaughter
aligned with the family of that mushroom! Never! Not as
long as I have breath in my body."

As a result of the shouted threats, a sobbing Lilia fled
to her bedchamber, locking the door behind her and refus-
ing to come out even when begged to do so by her mother.
Meanwhile, Andrew quit the bookroom and came to find
his brother. Angrier than anyone had ever seen him before,
he begged Zach to accompany him to Blinbourne, to the
Dancing Bear.

"I must regain control of my temper," he said. "And to
do so, I must get away from Gillmore House. I cannot remain here for one more minute. Otherwise, I might say
something I will regret for a very long time."

"Of course," Zach replied. "Go to the stable and have
the horses saddled, then wait for me there. I will have small
bags packed for us for tonight. The remainder of our things

can be fetched on the morrow when the coachman comes
for the chaise."

After his brother left, Zach gave Judith one long, searching look, then he quit the room.

The tap room of the Dancing Bear was filled to capacity,
as was the inn itself. Due to the pending race meet, the
brothers had been obliged to share a bedchamber, though
they were fortunate enough to procure a private table in
the public room.

"The old martinet must think himself a monarch of some
kind," Andrew said, "to order me about and expect me to
fall in with his plans."

His brother nodded his agreement with the statement,
though it was not the first time he had heard it since their
departure from Gillmore House.

"I tell you, Zach, if it were not for our having met the
ladies, I could wish we had never answered the summons
to come down to Dorset for the fortnight."

Zach was in wholehearted agreement with this observation, for these past two weeks had left his usually stoic
brain in a turmoil. Though in all honesty it was not the
weeks that had cut up his peace, nor the coming to Dorset.
It was Judith Preston!

Never before had any woman occupied so much of
Zach's thoughts—both waking and sleeping—occupied
them to the exclusion of all rational consideration. Not that
he faulted Judith for that. Far from it, for his admiration of
her seemed to grow with each new day. She was a young
lady eminently worthy of respect. He admired her for her
sincere concern for her mother and sister, and for her love
and devotion to them and to the memory of her stepfather.

Honest and genuine, she was a totally natural person.

When she loved, the wood nymph gave her all, feigning nothing. So real. So unspoiled. So genuine. So desirable!

It was this last recollection that caused Zach to rake his fingers through his hair in frustration. If only he had not kissed her. If he had done as he vowed and kept his hands to himself, he would never have experienced her receptiveness to his attempts at amour—receptiveness so sweet and warm it had needed all his resolve just to move away from her. If he had never tasted of that warmth, that sweetness, he might have been able to leave Dorset whole of heart. Maybe.

"Zach," Andrew said, leaning across the table and speaking in a whisper, "you will never guess who is sitting just behind you."

Forcing his thoughts back to the present, Zach said, "Must I guess? With the place filled to overflowing with humanity, it could be anyone. I daresay if a fellow looked close enough, he might discover any number of acquaintances lurking in the corners."

"Shh," Andrew cautioned, "lower your voice, for they are no acquaintances of mine. Not unless our having partaken of breakfast at the same time and in the same inn in Dorcester qualifies as an introduction."

"I am in no mood for riddles, lad, so if—"

"It is those two black legs I saw that morning almost two weeks ago, when we first traveled into Dorset. You remember, I told you about my overhearing them discussing the race meet."

"Ah, yes. The little man with the pink scalp and the big fellow whose neck you likened to that of an ox."

Andrew nodded. "The little one is mere inches from you. If you were to lean back, you might be able to hear what he is saying."

"Firstly," Zach said, "the noise level in this room makes

it difficult for a man to hear his own thoughts, never mind someone else's conversation. Secondly, I have no interest in knowing what the fellow has to say."

"You may when I tell you that I caught a snatch of something just a moment ago, and unless I am very much mistaken, the little man mentioned Stanbury's Bess."

"Young Rainsford's horse?"

Offering no more objections, Zach lifted the empty pewter tankard that sat before him. Leaning back so that the chair was balanced on its back legs, he pretended to down the last dregs of the ale.

Even with his ear very near the speaker, he heard only pieces of the conversation.

"Entered 'er late, 'e did, but I 'ear tell she's the likeliest filly of the lot. 'A real sweet goer,' 'er jockey says. A Pegasus, with wings on 'er 'ooves."

A sudden burst of laughter from the far end of the room rendered the next few comments unintelligible, and the next bit of conversation Zach could understand had to do with the betting odds on each filly.

"Odds is going in Bess's favor, and rising by the hour."

Zach lost another entire patch of conversation, but the final remarks were worrisome enough to put him on his mettle.

"We'll sit tight until early Friday," the man said, "let the odds soar even 'igher. Then, when most of the wagers is set, we'll do what 'as to be done to bring things right."

The fellow with the oxen neck finally spoke. " 'Ow you want I should take care of the 'orse? Summit in 'er feed, or—"

"Stubble it," the smaller man muttered, then he turned slightly as though becoming aware of Zach leaning close.

To allay suspicion, Zach sat forward, letting the front legs of his chair hit the floor with a loud *thump*. After placing the empty tankard on the table, he said, "I'm for bed." He tossed several coins beside the tankard, then he pushed his chair back, standing none too steadily, and nearly toppling over onto the table.

"Think I need a bit of a hand," he said to his startled brother. "I seem to have exceeded my limit. Don't believe I can manage the stairs unassisted."

After a moment's stunned silence, Andrew's wide-eyed expression relaxed. Obviously perceiving the purpose of the charade, he pushed his own chair back then hurried around to stand beside his brother.

"By jove!" he said, "didn't realize you had gotten so disguised." Catching Zach's arm, he began leading him toward the door. "Here, lean on me, there's a good fellow."

As the smaller man led the larger from the tap room, the blackleg's interest waned, and he dismissed them out of hand. In such a crowded room, what was one more inebriate?

Early the next morning, while Zach and Andrew broke their fast before riding over to the race course to apprise Stan Rainsford of what they had overheard in the tap room, Miss Judith Preston rose from her bed, applied cold compresses to her eyes to hide the fact that she had not slept a wink the night before, then dressed herself for a walk to Rainsford Manor.

It had been the longest night of her life, with her emotions in utter chaos as she speculated upon the chance of her ever seeing Zachery Camden again. Would he return? And if so, when? The way he had quit Gillmore House, leaving without vouchsafing even one word of farewell to her, there was a distinct possibility that he might never come back.

"Fate must be toying with the Preston family," she told the ashen face in the looking glass. "Your father could not win at faro, and you seem destined to lose at the game of hearts."

Judith laughed at her little joke, but there was no joy in the face of her reflection. "Shall I tell you your problem?" she asked that wan visage. "You are just not lucky. How ironic that the moment you admitted to yourself how much you loved Zachery Camden, and that you would ask nothing more of life than to be allowed to chance your destiny with his, he went away. Just like that! As quickly as one turns over a card on a green baize table."

"Judith," Lilia called from the other room, her voice still thick with sleep, "who are you talking to?"

"Myself. Forgive me. I did not mean to wake you."

"You sound strange. Are you unwell?"

"No. I am fine. Truly. Go back to sleep."

When her sister said no more, Judith took one last peek into the looking glass, then she did something she had not done since she was a child, she made an ogre face and stuck out her tongue. "That is what I think of your crying and moaning, Judith Preston. Now stop whining about a situation that cannot be helped, and do something constructive! Go talk to Sir Thomas."

Having given her reflection what for, she grabbed her yellow chip straw hat, tied it gypsy fashion beneath her chin, then left the room.

Her wounded heart notwithstanding, Judith found it a lovely morning for a walk. The lane was dry, making patents unnecessary, and the sky was a clear blue with only a scattering of little woolen clouds for accent. A soft balmy breeze blew at her back, and when she breathed deeply, she fancied she could smell the waves that dashed against the shore at Durdle Door.

She walked briskly, enjoying the exercise, and wishing it might last for some time. Unfortunately, that was not to be, for once she passed through the entrance gates of Gillmore House, it was scarcely more than a mile to the gravel carriageway at Rainsford Manor.

No less than Andrew was Judith astounded at her first view of the ornate brick mansion Sir Thomas had caused to be constructed as a monument to his success. Stopping before the portico, she spared a moment to stare at the profusion of gargoyles before turning her attention to the intricately carved motto above the heavy oak entrance doors.

"Impressive, ain't it?" Sir Thomas said, startling Judith by appearing just behind her on the carriageway, as if materializing from thin air.

Not wishing to give offense by owning the truth of her first impression of the house, she chose to misunderstand him. "I fear I do not read Latin, sir."

"Me neither," replied the gentleman, removing his wide-brimmed straw hat and shaking Judith's proffered hand, "but it adds a bit of class. Don't you think?"

Forcing a lame smile, she said, "Latin is certainly classical."

Sir Thomas pushed open his bottle green coat and hooked his thumbs in the small pockets of his brightly stripped gold waistcoat. "What say you, Miss Preston, of the house itself?"

"I . . . er, say that I never see a house such as this without thinking how much a few well-planted rose bushes would add to the charm of its aspect."

Sir Thomas seemed much struck by the idea. "Roses,

eh? Leave it to a female to think of prettifying a place with flowers."

Her host seemed to recall his manners and asked if she would care to step inside for a dish of tea. Since Judith had come alone, and there was no hostess at Rainsford Manor, she declined the offer in favor of a walk to the stables. "I understand they are magnificent."

"Heard that from Miss Lilia, did you?"

"From Lieutenant Gillmore, actually. However, now you have mentioned my sister, I think I shall not waste the introduction of the subject, but get directly to the point of my visit."

Sir Thomas paused, though the stables were still some distance away, and looked directly at Judith, the expression on his ruddy face a fine blend of shrewdness and injured sensibility held in check. "Wisest to get over rough terrain as quickly as possible, I always say. I gather you have come to discuss this crazy notion the two young people have gotten into their nous boxes."

"I have, sir."

"Not that you need to tell me how the idea was received at Gillmore House, for I can guess his lordship's reaction. If the liaison had been deemed acceptable to him, he would have paid me a visit himself, him being the young lady's grandfather, and the properest person to call."

Embarrassed that Sir Thomas perceived her visit as a slight, Judith said, "Lord Gillmore never does the *proper* thing, sir, only that thing which best suits his own purpose. As for me, I have come because there is a question I would ask."

"Well, now, miss, pleased as I am to have you visit, I'll tell you to your head that marriage contracts ain't the kind of thing a man usually discusses with a female."

"No, no. This has nothing to do with the business of

marriage, Sir Thomas. What I want to know—what I need to know—is if you mean to put a stumbling block in the way of this betrothal. I understand that at one time you entertained hopes of a more advantageous alliance for your son—one with a young lady of more elevated social connections than my sister—and if you still cherish that same ambition, I should like to know it so that I may protect Lilia from heartache. All other considerations aside, I would see her happy in her life's choice."

Sir Thomas looked Judith over, taking her measure, much as he would scrutinize a horse whose temper he did not know. Finally he said, "Your devotion to your sister does you credit, Miss Preston, and since you have been forthright with me, I will do the same by you."

"Please do."

"My boy is very independent in his thinking, and though he's a soft-spoken lad, he's nonetheless sure of what he wants. For instance, I wanted him to be a gentleman, to go about town a bit to hobnob with his school chums and enjoy some of my money, but Stan wanted no part of that scheme. He had his heart set on raising thoroughbreds, and I guess you know which one of us won that argument."

Judith nodded.

"As for tomorrow's race meet, I was opposed to it from the start, and I figured if I withheld the money needed to enter, that would be the end of it. As you see, I was wrong again. The lad found the money elsewhere and left me out of the picture."

It was not difficult to see that the man was hurt by this minor defection by his only child, and Judith felt compassion for him. "I am sorry, Sir Thomas."

"You are very kind, miss, but it was my own fault, for I misjudged my man. I won't do that again. And, of course, you are right when you say this betrothal ain't what I would have chosen. However, my son tells me he loves Miss Lilia, and a man only has to look into the lad's eyes to see he means it. Stan is all the family I've got, and knowing how he feels, and how independent he is, I would be a fool to raise objections that would surely come between us."

He bid her turn and look once again at the house. "I built the place big enough to accommodate a large family, and I pray that one day I'll see the nursery filled to overflowing. If Stan and Miss Lilia make a match of it, I mean to welcome her as mistress of the house, and I will see she is given all the respect and honor due my son's chosen wife and the mother of my grandchildren." He cleared his throat. "And I hope that answers your questions about me putting any stumbling blocks in the way of this marriage."

"It does," Judith said, her voice just a bit unsteady. "And if I may say so, Sir Thomas, I think my sister is very fortunate in her choice of father-in-law. You are a very wise man, and I look forward to becoming better acquainted with you. That is, if I am invited to visit that nursery full of nieces and nephews."

"Invited?" Sir Thomas said, his florid face beaming with pleasure, "no invitation needed, my dear, for you'll be family. Come early and stay late, as the saying goes. You and your mama both. Can't ever have too much company to suit me."

Twelve

"Was that all he said?" Stan asked Zach. "That he would do what had to be done to bring things right?"

"That is all I heard. That and the oxen-necked fellow's question about how his confederate wanted him to take care of the horse."

Stan balled his hands into fists then began to pace the paddock. They had chosen not to remain in the dim, rather cramped area allotted each owner for his horse and tack, and had gone instead to the paddock, an area where the horses would be saddled and paraded before the race. It was as well, for Stan looked as though he needed to pace, in hopes of relieving some of his anger.

Leaving the young man to his thoughts, Zach joined his brother who leaned against the split-rail fence, watching one of the hopeful entrants, a pretty gray filly, being exercised.

"What did he say?" Andrew asked, not taking his eyes from the likely looking three-year-old who was being put through her paces.

"Very little," Zach replied. "Young Rainsford is a man of few words. But judging by the intimidating size of the two grooms who are guarding Bess, I suspect the lad was prepared for something like this."

"So all is well?"

Zach did not answer immediately. "It would appear so, but truth to tell, I have a bad feeling about this. If you should not dislike it too much, Andrew, I would prefer to remain in Dorset another day. At least until after the race."

From the big smile on the young man's face, the suggestion obviously suited him. "By jove, Zach, you must know my answer to that, for the race meet was the one thing I was looking forward to during this fortnight."

Abandoning his examination of the gray filly, Andrew moved closer to his brother so they might speak without being overheard. "What do you propose we do?"

"We?"

Andrew gave his brother a long-suffering look. "Naturally I mean *we*. Surely you do not expect me to return to the inn and wait patiently for the race. I want to be part of the adventure."

"Adventure?" Zach smiled at his brother's still-youthful exuberance. "What I have planned will hardly rate as that, but I have no objection to your being involved in it."

"Capital!"

"I agree with young Rainsford," Zach continued, "that guarding the horse seems the only sensible precaution. She should eat and drink nothing that is not procured for her by one of the grooms, and no stranger should be allowed within several feet of her stall. That being the accepted regimen, I propose merely to spell the grooms for a few hours this evening so they may get some much needed rest. If you wish to join me, you may, though the whole will probably involve nothing more than sitting in a corner of the stall until your knees stiffen on you like an old man's."

Like a soldier volunteering for a dangerous mission, Andrew's tone was serious. "I shall be happy to do whatever is necessary." That said, he spoiled the whole by grinning boyishly. "As long," he amended, "as the task does not involve a shovel."

Zach laughed. "Too top-lofty to muck a stall, eh, Lieutenant?"

"Have no fear, Gillmore," Stan said, joining them in time to hear a portion of their conversation, "I appreciate your willingness to help far too much to ask you to do anything so demeaning. Besides," he continued, winking at Zach, "we would not want you to do anything that would mar those pretty new Hessians."

Andrew took the teasing in good part, and after the three gentlemen had spent a few minutes making arrangements to spell the grooms, Zach left the two younger men arguing the merits of the gray filly, in very good spirits with one another.

Zach needed some time to himself, for he had not had a moment for private thought since last evening when they quit Gillmore House. Their departure had been so abrupt, and under such high drama, that he had not been able to speak privately with Judith.

Not that she had appeared all that desirous of his company. As a matter of fact, she had been uncharacteristically quiet at dinner, and even while her sister played upon the pianoforte, she had seemed distant, as though lost in thought. Or angry.

Could she still be angry with him over that scene in the garden? He had thought they had made up; especially after she had responded with such warmth and sweetness to his kiss.

The kiss! Was that it?

Was Judith regretting her response to him? Females were raised differently from men, and as a consequence, they took such things as kisses much more seriously. Was she supposing that he would think less of her now? Afraid she might be supposing just that, he determined to ride over to Gillmore House to speak with her that very morning.

He would inform her, without any roundaboutation, that he respected and admired her more than any other female he had ever met, and that her friendship was very important to him. Would always be important to him! Then he would assure her that he wished her every happiness in the future.

Unfortunately, the thought that such happiness might involve her kissing some other man made Zach's hands curl into fists. He pictured her at some time in the future; she was in that other man's arms, allowing that other man to hold her soft, yielding body close to his. Then he saw her surrendering to the cad her lips, her warm response, even her innocence, and Zach found himself with a totally unreasonable desire to put his fist through someone's face.

Someone? Damnation! He wanted to punch that imaginary fellow's lights out!

Still seething from the image he had conjured out of his own head, he determined to speak with Judith immediately, to warn her against bestowing herself upon one who was unworthy of her. With that thought in mind, he marched over to the field where the visitors' horses were held, tossed a coin to the startled groom, and all but leapt upon the back of his black gelding.

What Lieutenant Gillmore and Stan Rainsford thought of his riding away, without so much as a word of farewell, Zach neither knew nor cared. Suffice it to say, that when those two young gentlemen witnessed the angry scowl wrinkling Zach's brow, and his abrupt, rather dramatic leave-taking, they assumed it concerned a matter of some importance: ergo, something to do with tomorrow's race.

* * *

Arriving at the narrow lane that sloped upward from the main road, giving access to Gillmore House, Zach slowed the gelding from a gallop to a trot. Always before, the magnificent view had moved Zach, with the green hills of the downs to his left, and to his right the distant scarps that plunged to the Channel below. But not today. Today he rode with a purpose in mind, and that objective was his pending conversation with Miss Judith Preston.

As luck would have it, just as he neared the iron gates that guarded the carriageway of Gillmore House, he met the object of his gallop from Blinbourne; she was approaching him from the opposite direction. To his frustration, she was not alone, but rode beside Sir Thomas Rainsford, the two of them squeezed rather snugly into an ancient pony trap.

To Zach's further annoyance, Judith was laughing at something the widower had said. Not smiling politely in a ladylike manner, but tossing her head back and giving vent to her mirth in a way that must make any gentleman—never mind his total unsuitability, or the fact that he was old enough to be her father—feel she was interested in him.

Spying the rider, Sir Thomas reined in the pony just outside the gate and waited for Zach. "Well met, Mr. Camden," he greeted affably. "Is this not a glorious day?"

"Quite," he answered, though even that concession to civility tasted bitter upon his tongue.

"Zach," Judith said, the laughter of a moment ago gone as though it had never been. "I thought . . . that is, I was not certain that you and your brother were still in the neighborhood."

"We are put up at the Dancing Bear. For the moment, at least."

"A comfortable inn," Sir Thomas said. "Take my advice, sir, and try the roast lamb. They have a way with it there."

Before Zach could reply in a civil manner, he saw the old lecher pat Judith's hand where it rested upon the handle of a wicker basket.

"What do you think of this young lady?" he asked with a familiarity that made Zach want to yank the presumptuous fellow right out of the cart. "Is she not a good sport to allow me to give her a lift in such a disreputable piece of equipage?"

"A very good sport," Zach agreed, his jaw clenched so tightly the words were almost unintelligible.

"Of course," Sir Thomas continued, "I saw fit to bribe her first."

He pointed to the basket that reposed upon Judith's lap. "Cook had just made a batch of almond tarts, and when Miss Preston told me they were her favorite sweet, I insisted she take some home with her."

Sir Thomas laughed as though he had told a good joke, but Zach was not to know if Judith was similarly amused, for she lowered her head, effectively hiding her face behind the wide brim of her gypsy hat.

Quite put out by the older man's jocularity, Zach said, "Too many sweet treats will spoil animals and young ladies alike."

At his sharp tone, Judith looked up, but it was the widower who spoke. "Not Miss Preston," he declared. "How could anything spoil such a sweet, unaffected young lady?"

When Judith's cheeks grew pink, Sir Thomas patted her hand again. "Forgive me, my dear, for putting you to the blush. You may say I've no more feeling than an old shoe, and you'd be in the right of it. Been living like a bachelor far too long, don't you know. Need a woman's refining touch."

At this last remark, he winked at Judith. "Not but what that'll be mended soon enough, I've no doubt."

Judith made no reply, but looked over at Zach, her blue eyes more serious than he had ever seen them. "Shall we see you at the races tomorrow?" she asked.

"We?"

"Yes," Sir Thomas answered for her. "Miss Preston has agreed to give me the pleasure of her company tomorrow. It looks like being another wonderful day, and since she tells me her mama has put off her blacks, I am hoping to persuade her and Miss Lilia to join us. But lest you think I mean to squeeze them all into the pony cart, I'll tell you that I gave orders to have the landau cleaned and polished and made as neat as any lady could require. Of course, my old landau is not the equal to that bang-up chaise of yours, but with the hoods down, the ladies will have a good view of Stanbury's Bess when she wins the race."

"I hope you may be right," Zach said.

Watching his unsmiling face, Judith had no idea whether Zach's hopes were for the view the ladies would have of the race, or for the identity of the race's winner. The latter, she supposed. After all, he had risked eight hundred pounds upon the outcome. The money was probably his reason for remaining in the neighborhood.

Perhaps his only reason.

Though she did not wish to admit the possibility that it was not *she* who had inspired Zach to stay in Dorset, it was better to face the facts. Better not to delude herself. Though when all was said and done, honesty offered little comfort to her heart.

Swallowing her pride, she forced a smile to her lips then said, "Will you come up to the house, Zach? Sir Thomas has expressed an interest in seeing the picture gallery, and he has consented to remain for a cup of tea. Please join us."

When he shook his head, she held up the basket containing the almond tarts. "You may share in my decadence."

"No, I thank you, madam. Some other time, perhaps."

"Yes," she replied, her throat practically choked with the tears at his curt refusal. "Some other time."

Sir Thomas said something that Judith did not hear, but whatever it was it must have served as a parting remark, for Zach lifted his hat in farewell, turned the gelding, and galloped off down the lane.

Surprisingly, their neighbor did not encourage the pony to be on his way. Instead, he left the reins slack, his attention fixed upon Mr. Camden until that gentleman disappeared from view. "A good seat," he said. "And good hands. Knows how to handle a lively horse without breaking his spirits."

"Yes," Judith replied, though the last thing she wanted to discuss with him was Zachery Camden.

"And a real gentleman," Sir Thomas continued. "A swell, as the young men say. Stylish in his dress, a man of social position, and distinguished in his career."

Before Judith could ask him what he meant by *career*—surely not even Sir Thomas would call gambling more than a pastime—he asked her something that put the entire question from her mind.

"Have you and Mr. Camden an understanding?"

Judith very nearly choked. "An under—"

"Take my advice," he added with a wink, "the gentleman would make you a fine husband."

"No, no. There is nothing like that, sir, I assure you."

"Odd," replied the widower, "for I would have bet my last groat that the gentleman was interested in you. Otherwise, why was he looking as though he'd like to put a bullet through my heart?"

While Judith tried to assimilate this last piece of information, Sir Thomas lifted the reins, encouraging the pony through the wrought-iron gates and up the gravel carriage-way.

"Yes," he continued, almost to himself, "either I'm no judge of men, or that young fellow was jealous."

Zach stretched his long legs, hoping a new position might alleviate the stiffness caused from sitting on the hard, unyielding floor. He had relieved the grooms less than two hours ago, but his knees and backside felt as though they had been wedged into the corner of the cramped stall for the entire night. And it did not help his disposition any that his mind kept returning to his encounter with Judith and Sir Thomas Rainsford.

An interest in seeing the picture gallery! Ha!

As if that old reprobate would know a Hogarth from a hole in the ground.

Zach was livid. He had been livid for most of the day. And with good reason! How dare Judith take Sir Thomas up to the gallery. The place was special to her, and Zach had come to think of it as special to them both. Just like the weir, or the stretch of beach beneath the chalk cliffs, or the sheep path that ended at the kissing gate.

"Zach!" Andrew hissed. "For the love of Heaven, stop mumbling under your breath. You are frightening the horse, and for all I know, alerting anyone on the other side of the door that we are in here."

"Your pardon," Zach replied, keeping his voice at a whisper. "My thoughts were otherwhere."

Not placated, Andrew said, "I thought the whole point of our being here was to surprise any villains who might wish to injure Bess. If I have mistaken the matter, however, please say so, for I would love to stretch my own limbs. Perhaps go into the paddock and walk around a bit."

Zach understood his brother's show of temper. He could do with a turn outside himself. It was not bad enough that the stall measured no more than ten by ten; in addition, the door was closed tightly so that not a breath of fresh air got to the filly.

Young Rainsford's thinking on the treatment of horses was radical by present standards, in that he did not prescribe to the prevalent theories regarding severe sweats and purges for his animals, but he did insist that Bess be protected from the threat of the night air. As a result, it was the two gentlemen guarding the horse who suffered from the heat.

"If you are tired, Andrew, why not go outside for a few minutes. I can stand watch alone long enough for you to take a turn around the paddock."

"No, I will stay. You—"

"Shh!" Zach said.

Both men fell silent, for someone had stopped outside the stall and was even now sliding a thin, flat tool of some kind beneath the door and up the side.

Without making a sound, Zach rose to his feet, his senses suddenly alert, for within a very few seconds the tool had found its way beneath the wooden bar and was lifting it free of the notch.

Slowly the door was pushed wide and a giant of a man stood in the opening. Though it was quite dark inside, there was enough light for Zach to recognize the blackleg with the ox's neck, and enough to reveal the thing he held in his hand. It was a pistol, and it was pointed directly at Andrew's chest.

"Don't move, lad," the man said, squinting into the darkness. "Stay right there on the floor, and won't nobody get 'urt. I'm gonna give the filly a little summit to eat, is all, and I'd advise you not to try and stop me. Just a nice lump of sugar. It won't do 'her no real 'arm, and by this time tomorrow, she'll be good as new."

He stepped closer to Andrew, obviously unaware that Zach stood in the other corner. "Do yourself a favor, lad, and turn a blind eye. You cooperate, and there might even be a bob or two in it for you."

Before Andrew had time to reply to the man's attempted bribe, Zach rushed forward, a shovel raised above his head. In an instant, he had brought the tool down hard on the man's arm, the metal of the scoop clanking against the metal of the pistol and sending it flying across the small space to land somewhere in the hay. Though the man was practically unfazed by what should have been a stunning blow, he took one look at Zach, the shovel raised to strike again, then he turned and fled into the night.

As soon as the villain was gone, Andrew hurried to the door, slammed it shut and slipped the bar back into the notch. "Whew," he said leaning his back against the rough wood, his breathing coming fast, as though he had run several miles.

"Good man," Zach said. "You kept your head about you."

Ignoring the compliment, he said, "Do you see the pistol? The scoundrel dropped it quite close to your foot."

After poking the strewn hay with the toe of his boot, Zach bent down and lifted something. "Yes," he replied, "I have it."

"Good. Then pass me the shovel."

Zach chuckled suddenly. "If I remember correctly, Lieutenant Gillmore, when you were so magnanimous as to volunteer for this mission, you said you would be happy to do whatever was necessary, as long as the task did not involve a shovel."

"That was this morning," Andrew replied. "As of a minute ago, I changed my mind."

Thirteen

Sir Thomas's coachman deftly maneuvered the perfectly matched grays and the recently polished landau into one of the few remaining spaces. Satisfied with the spot, he signaled for one of the urchins who waited hopefully at the sidelines to come stand at the horses' heads.

To the left of their space was a flashy yellow phaeton bearing two slightly inebriated young gentlemen—gentlemen their host quickly stigmatized as "young puppies"—and to the right was a handsome maroon open carriage occupied by a family party consisting of two fashionably dressed young ladies, a gentleman who must have been their older brother, and a schoolboy perhaps thirteen years old.

The coachman had been fortunate to find a space, for conveyances of every kind filled the area. As well, every available tree had been staked out by lads who perched on limbs Judith sincerely hoped would prove strong enough to bear their weight. One of the townsmen, an enterprising fellow had even built a scaffold some fifteen or so feet high and was charging the tulips of the turf a shilling per man for the privilege of climbing aboard.

"So many people," Mrs. Gillmore said. "I cannot credit the number who are here already. Surely it wants more than an hour before the race begins?"

Thankfully, Sir Thomas made some sort of reply to her mother's observation, for Judith was far too busy scanning the throng of gentlemen, villagers, and strangers of varying social status who sauntered about greeting friends, consulting their racing sheets, and visiting the betting ring.

Where was Zach? Had he come early, in hopes of acquiring a good viewing spot, or was he still at the inn?

Judith had spent another sleepless night, but this time her inability to find repose resulted not from a bruised heart, but from the anticipation of seeing Zach on the morrow. Had Sir Thomas been correct? she asked herself a hundred times before daybreak. Could Zach have been acting like a jealous man?

Not that he had any reason to be jealous. Nor did she wish to give him any cause to be. But, oh, if he felt even a twinge of that unpleasant feeling, it could only mean that he harbored other feelings as well—feelings not unlike those Judith held inside her own heart.

She was brought to a sense of where she was by a sudden sharp poke in the ribs. "Judith," Lilia whispered, "is that Cousin Andrew I see over there? If it is, try if you can get his attention, for I want to ask him to escort us to the stalls. I want to wish Stan *bon chance*."

Hoping that Zach might be with his brother, Judith was happy to obey her sister's instructions. After searching the crowded area Lilia indicated, letting her gaze skip from one gentleman's head to another, she finally spotted Lieutenant Gillmore's dark blond hair.

He had stopped at a smart-looking curricle where two young gentlemen in military uniform greeted him with enthusiasm, pumping his hand, and banging him on the shoulder as though quite pleased to have encountered an old friend. Andrew seemed equally pleased to see them, and when he turned aside, beckoning someone to join him, Judith finally got her wish, for the person who appeared was Zach.

Looking more handsome than she had ever seen him, he wore a coat of Spanish blue that fit his muscular frame to perfection, and when he removed his curly-brimmed beaver hat and bowed politely to the military gentlemen, the sun shone upon his black hair, making it glisten like the pelt of a panther. Though Judith wished Zach had come straight to Sir Thomas's carriage, she contented herself with watching him as he shook hands with his brother's two friends.

However, it was another matter altogether when he was hailed a moment later by a middle-aged gentleman whose ebony and gold carriage bore a crest upon the door. The gentleman's companion was a flaxen-haired beauty in emerald green jaconet, and the lady—if that was what she was—made no attempt to conceal her appreciation of Zach's good looks. After laughing at something he said, she leaned quite close to him and whispered something in his ear.

At Zach's response, she pouted winsomely then rapped him on the arm with her fan.

"La, sir," Judith heard her exclaim, "you cannot mean to leave me with only my husband for escort? That is most unkind of you, and if we should meet at Lady Dawling's next week, do not expect me to have saved a place for your name on my dance card."

Judith did not hear Zach's response, but he put his hand upon his heart as though wounded, then he made the pair an elegant bow. It was while he was raising his head that his gaze met hers.

Cool gray locked with medium blue, and for a moment it seemed as though he and she were the only two people at the racecourse. Nay, the only two people in the world.

Still beset by doubts about Zach's feelings, Judith chanced a smile, and he answered with that slow, mocking tug at the corner of his mouth—a tug that soon became a genuine smile. Unfortunately, Sir Thomas chose that very moment to reach out and shoo away a furry bee fly that hovered above the violets Judith had pinned to the brim of her French bonnet, and when Zach spied her host, his smile became a scowl.

Almost immediately, he concealed that display of emotion by donning the mask Judith had witnessed on other occasions, but the scowl had lasted long enough for her to see it. See it and realize its significance. Sir Thomas was correct; Zachery Camden was jealous!

Judith felt her face flush with pleasure, and she was still trying to conceal the betraying sign when Zach bid farewell to the flaxen-haired beauty then approached the landau, bowing to one and all.

"Mrs. Gillmore," he said, lifting her mother's hand almost to his lips, "a pleasure to see you, ma'am. May I say how charmingly that blue becomes you?"

"Told her that myself," Sir Thomas said affably, if a bit loudly. Then lowering his voice he added, "But the lady is feeling a bit shy about being out of her black in public."

"I am twice a widow," the lady said quietly, "and for that reason, such compliments as are appropriate should be paid my daughters."

Sir Thomas rolled his eyes heavenward. "I ask you, Mr. Camden, did you ever hear such fustian? As if this pair of chits—comely though they may be—can hold a candle to their mother."

Dorothy Gillmore blushed prettily, and Zach, apparently seeking the answer to a puzzle, looked directly at Sir Thomas. Judith could not discern if he found what he sought, but a moment later he took Mrs. Gillmore's hand again, this time raising it to his lips and placing a kiss upon her fingers. "Sir Thomas is correct, ma'am. You are truly a rose between two thorns."

"Well!" Lilia protested, though a giggle gave the lie to her outrage. "For such a *compliment* as that, sir, I shall insist you make restitution by giving me your escort to the paddock. The other thorn and I wish to view the fillies before the race."

Amid the laughter of the others, Zach said, "My pleasure, Miss Lilia."

He helped Lilia from the carriage, then he turned to offer his hand to Judith, giving her a slow teasing smile that all but took her breath away. "And what of you, Miss Thorn? Will you grant me the honor of your company?"

"Yes," she said, "I will."

The paddock where the fillies were being paraded for view looked surprisingly festive, for colorful bunches of flowers had been tied to the split-rail fence that surrounded the area. The entrants, too, were dressed for the occasion, and Stanbury's Bess, led by one of the grooms, wore across her back a satin blanket in a checkered pattern of carmine and white. Stan's colors had only just been registered with The Jockey Club, and the blanket was a match to the jockey's newly arrived silks.

"Oh," Lilia said, her face beaming with pride, "just look at Bess. Is she not splendid?"

"A winner all the way," Zach said.

Judith gave it as her opinion that they were both correct, then she asked if they might find a viewing spot that was a little less crowded. Dozens of men were still trying to guess the possible winner from among the entrants, and Judith had no desire to have her new kid boots trod upon.

As the threesome moved further down the paddock fence, Judith noticed a half-dozen jockeys, already dressed in their bright silks, congregated near the tall boxwood hedge that separated the paddock from the stalls area. Each rider wore the colors of the gentleman whose horse he would race, the silks making them appear even slimmer than they actually were. Because horses ran faster with a lighter load, jockies were hired not only for their riding skill, but also for their weight, or lack thereof.

The riders were mostly in their mid to late twenties—full-grown men, every one of them—but they were all unusually short, only one of them appearing even as tall as Judith. They were talking excitedly among themselves, and from the way they kept their voices down, she had a feeling their excitement involved more than prerace nerves.

Judith was not the only one to notice the group, and as Lilia stared at the men, her face suddenly turned ashen. "Something is amiss," she said, clutching at Zach's coat sleeve. "May we go to the stalls, sir? Please, I must see Stan immediately, for I believe he needs me."

Because Lilia would not be calmed otherwise, Zach led the two women to the stall where he knew Stan would be waiting. After one look at that young man's face, Lilia flew into his arms.

"What has happened?" Zach asked.

Stan pointed to the carmine and white silks that lay neatly folded across the stall door, silks that should already have been donned. "We guarded the horse," he said soberly, "but we forgot about the jockey."

Zach muttered something beneath his breath. "Where is he now?"

"At the Dancing Bear. Someone entered his room in the early hours of the morning and left him severely beaten."

In frustration, Zach slammed the flat of his hand against

the wooden door, making them all jump. "This is my fault. I should have thought of that possibility. Especially after Mr. Ox Neck gave up so easily on the filly."

Judith knew a moment of fear, for it was obvious to her that there had been a confrontation of some sort at the stalls the night before. And just as obvious that Zach had had some part in it. Had he been injured?

"How badly is Ziegler hurt?" he asked.

"The apothecary is seeing to him right now," Stan said, "but his chances of riding today do not look promising."

"Mr. Autry is a skilled healer," Judith said, offering what hope she could. "Perhaps he can patch Mr. Ziegler sufficiently for the race."

Stan cleared his throat. "Ziegler may have a broken rib. If so, a ride could prove fatal."

Lilia began to sob softly against Stan's shoulder. "What are we to do now?"

"There is nothing we can do, my love. It is much too late to find another jockey, for the gong sounds within the next ten minutes. If our man is not dressed and on the horse within two minutes after the sound of the gong, I not only lose the race, I face a penalty fine. There is no help for it, I will be obliged to withdraw Bess from the race."

"What about one of the grooms?" Judith suggested. "They help in Bess's training, might one of them fill in?"

Stan shook his head. "The rider must wear silks registered with The Jockey Club. Those," he said, pointing to the white shirt and carmine breeches, "were made to fit Ziegler, who is five foot five and weighs nine stone. The grooms are strapping fellows, both of them."

Zach placed his hand on Stan's shoulder. "Delay the withdrawal until the very last second, lad. In the meantime, I will take a look-in at the Dancing Bear and see how your man is coming along."

Judith watched Zach hurry away, then she turned back to her future brother-in-law. "What happens if you must withdraw?"

"This late," he replied, "I will lose the full amount of the entrance fee. As well, all those who have wagered money on Bess to win the race will lose. Worse than the loss of the money, however, is the injury to my reputation as a breeder and as a racer."

Lilia gasped. "But none of this is your fault."

"True, but a last-minute withdrawal always looks suspicious, for the blacklegs have bribed breeders before. Since my horse is uninjured, there will be many who will suspect that I was in league with the legs."

"But you were not," Lilia protested.

"No, my love, but short of finding the villains and forcing them to confess that I had no part in their nefarious acts, there is no way that I can prove my innocence. If I were already an established breeder, perhaps I could weather the controversy, but as a beginner, I will be ruined before I have had an opportunity to start."

"Oh, Stan," Lilia cried. "What of our plans? Our dreams? If you do not win the race, how are we to be married?"

"Somehow," he said, holding her close, "we will be wed. But how, I wonder, am I to repay Mr. Camden his eight hundred pounds?"

Judith remembered reading somewhere that grand passions bred grand gestures. She believed hers to be a grand passion. But what of this plan? Was it a grand gesture, or merely a foolish act—one for which she might pay the rest of her life? If her ruse was discovered, the least that would happen to her would be social ostracism.

"Have courage," she said, pushing the possibility of disgrace from her mind. She would face that eventuality if and when it came, but for now, the reward was worth the risk.

After all, she could not let Stan's future—and with it her sister's happiness—be destroyed. Not when the saving of it was within her power. Not when she could ride as good as any man! And what of Zach, the man Judith loved with all her heart? He had said he could afford to lose the eight hundred pounds, but that was a great deal of money, and she would not stand idly by and watch him robbed of it.

When Stan and Lilia had gone to keep watch beside Bess, hoping against hope that Ziegler, the jockey, would appear before the starting time arrived, they had completely forgotten about Judith's presence. As if the two of them were alone, they had joined their hands in sad support, then they had left the stall and walked toward the paddock. It was while Judith watched them that the risky plan had come to her—full blown, as it were.

Instantly she had known she would—nay, she *must*—take the gamble.

The decision made, Judith removed her bonnet and gloves; then, crouching in the corner of the stall, where she could not be seen by any passersby, she undressed quickly, dropping her clothes—including her shift, her corset, and her drawers—into a pile upon the hay-strewn floor.

She thrust first one leg then the other into the carmine silk breeches, laced them snugly on either side, and double-tied the ribbon so there was no chance of the light-weight garment slipping off her hips. Ignoring the embarrassment that assailed her at the feel of men's breeches against her limbs, she bent and pulled her kid boots back on. The riding boots would not fit, but that was the least of her worries.

With fingers that were not quite steady, she wound the

cravat around her throat, tied it so the white silk shirt points were forced upward to shield her cheeks, then pulled the carmine-and-white-checkered jockey cap down low over her forehead.

Gong! the warning sounded the first time.

Gong! again.

Then, *Gongggggggg!*

The musical tone seemed to drone on forever. As Judith heard it fade into stillness, she planned aloud. "I now have two minutes in which to reach the filly, mount, and exit the paddock for the starting line. All without anyone opposing my actions."

It was both too little time and too much.

Hoping that if everything happened very fast, no one would get a good look at her, Judith began to count backwards. "Sixty. Fifty-nine. Fifty-eight. Fifty-seven." When she reached thirty, the replacement jockey stepped out of the concealing stall, took a deep, fortifying breath, and made a quick dash for the door.

Running as though her very life depended upon it, Judith sped down the gravel walk, whizzed past the boxwood hedge, and shoved open the paddock gate. She did not stop until she reached Bess, the only horse not already making its way toward the starting line.

"Toss me up," she instructed the startled groom.

"Here now," he said, turning toward the fence to seek guidance from his employer.

Afraid Bess's owner would realize she was not the rider he hired, Judith took a page from Lord Gillmore's book, and gave the hapless servant her most arrogant look. "Do as I say, you sapscull! And be quick about it!"

Reacting instinctively to the rough command, the groom yanked aside the blanket, grasped Judith's bent knee, and tossed her into the saddle.

"Ziegler!" she heard Stan yell from outside the fence. "Is that you?"

Judith knew she had mere seconds to spare before Stan became suspicious and vaulted the split-rail fence to seize his horse, so she snatched the reins from the second groom's hand and gave the filly a sharp kick in the sides.

Bess responded immediately, as though she knew the importance of the next eight to ten minutes, and had been waiting impatiently for someone to take charge. Trotting toward the starting line, her proud head held high, she took her place like the lady she was.

Two men dressed in brightly colored riding coats stood on either side of the track, a long white ribbon held taut between them, and it was behind this ribbon that the twenty fillies involved in the heat took their places. The instant all the animals were facing forward and ready, the men dropped the ribbon, and the official fired his pistol.

With no time to become accustomed to riding astride, Judith did as she had seen countless men do, she brought her knees in close to the filly's sides, leaned forward over Bess's neck, then pushed her weight into the stirrups and posted.

The four-mile heat had begun!

Zach arrived at the paddock fence just in time to hear young Rainsford yell Ziegler's name. Having hurried back from the inn to deliver the unpleasant news that the jockey definitely was not coming, Zach was no less surprised than Stan and Miss Lilia to see a rider wearing carmine and white silks rush forward and mount Stanbury's Bess.

As horse and rider trotted toward the starting line, Zach chanced to notice the way the breeches clung to the unknown jockey's slender, yet rounded posterior. Granted, in the past he had never paid any attention to that part of a jockey's anatomy, but in this instance there was some justification, for he was enough of a man of the world to recognize a female backside when he saw one.

And he had a horrible suspicion that he knew the owner of that particular backside!

Grabbing Stan's arm before the young man could hurry to the racecourse, he shouted, "Where is Judith?"

The lad struggled to pull free, impatient to be on his way. "She is here some place."

Zach would not unhand him. "Where?" he insisted.

Stan looked around him as if only that moment realizing that Lilia's sister was not with them. "Miss Preston must still be at the stall," he said, "but I feel certain she will come to no harm there. At any rate, sir, I beg you will let me go, for Ziegler has arrived, and I must see the race."

Zach lowered his voice so only Stan and Lilia could hear his words. "The rider is not Ziegler."

"But of course it is," Stan insisted. "Who else could it be?"

Lilia did not move. She was staring at Zach, her brown eyes beseeching him to reassure her. "Mr. Camden, do . . . do you think Judith gave the silks to some unknown jockey?"

"No," he replied, a finality in his voice. "I do not think she gave them to anyone."

Before he could say more, Lilia gasped. "No! It is not true. Judith would never do anything so shocking. She . . ."

The young lady whirled quickly to look toward the gathering horses and riders. She spied Bess, and for a moment she stood as stiff as a statue. "Judith," she whispered; then her hand went to her throat and she began to sway. Fortunately, Stan caught her before she fainted.

"Lilia, my love," he begged, "please, do not swoon. Not now. The race is beginning, and I must—"

"Rainsford!" Zach ordered, "take Miss Lilia to the stall. And be quick about it, for we have no time to lose."

"But the race," he said, torn between his love for his future bride and his desire to witness his horse in her first competition.

"The filly is in good hands," Zach said. "Win or lose, she will come to no harm. Accept my word upon that. Right now, it is Miss Preston we must worry about, for her reputation is in danger. Her reputation and your own."

Fourteen

Judith had always wanted to know how it would feel to ride without the restrictions of a skirt, and the limited mobility afforded by a side saddle. Now she knew. It was like flying!

It was obvious the filly possessed wings on her fetlocks, for in less than a minute they were in the front third of the pack. Sensing the animal's ability, Judith did not attempt to impose her will, but merely went along for the ride, content to let Bess choose her own speed. It proved to be a wise decision, for soon the horse settled into a steady, even gallop—an effortless pace that let them maintain a comfortable position just behind the ten front runners.

Midway the second of the four miles, three of the ten fillies who had surged ahead quickly began to slow. Lathered and blown, they lost ground with each successive gallop. While the trio faded and fell behind, Judith and Stanbury's Bess continued at their steady pace.

As they drew up beside a sleek, black-maned gray, the filly's jockey began to use his riding crop, whipping the animal's flanks to spur her to greater speed. Judith abhorred the practice of fanning, so she had left her crop behind. It was just as well, for if she had been in possession of it at the moment, she might have been tempted to fan the rider to give him a taste of his own treatment.

Soon the gray had given her all, and Judith and Bess were in seventh place.

As they rounded the curve that was the midway point of the course, they began to overtake a pair who appeared to be racing one another, running neck and neck.

"That's it, girl," Judith encouraged. "You can do it."

Flecks of foam spattered Judith's sleeves, and the thunderous stomping of hooves upon the hard ground sounded in her ears. Soon the noise of the hooves was lessened by eight as she and Bess pulled ahead of the pair.

Stanbury's Bess was now in fifth place.

Judith leaned even closer over the filly's neck, her knees all but touching, and her arms close in to her sides. Stealing a glance into the distance, she saw the fifteen-foot scaffold and the dozen or so tulips of the turf who clung to their handholds as they waved their hats and yelled encouragement.

"Go!" they screamed, almost as one. "Come on, you sweet beauty! Run!"

Seemingly spurred by their enthusiasm, Bess passed a chestnut and a roan with such ease they might as well have been standing still. Now there were only two horses ahead of her.

Judith and the filly might as well have been one, for she could literally feel the animal's desire to win. This was what Bess had been bred for. This was what she had been trained to do.

With less than half a mile to go, Judith felt something like a current surge through the horse's body. It was more than a bunching of the powerful muscles, much more than a stretching of the long, tapering legs. It was Bess's heart coming to life. Bess was a true champion, and as she sped down the final quarter mile, the champion's heart was beating within her, pumping energy into her hooves, filling her lungs with the pure air of victory.

Judith let the filly have her way, and with a motion as smooth and fluid as a brook, yet as forceful as the Channel waves that crashed against the rocks at Durdle Door, Bess pulled ahead, leaving the two lead horses to follow in her wake.

With her head down and her hooves pounding out a rhythmic beat upon the hard-packed earth of the track, the horse galloped so far out in front that she was virtually alone, all opponents vanquished. When she crossed the finish line, there was no doubt in anyone's mind as to who had won the heat, and the spectators cheered wildly, throwing their hats in the air and shouting "Hurray! Hurray!" for both horse and rider.

This was a race to go down in history, they yelled. This was a story to tell and retell, not only among themselves, but also to those not fortunate enough to have witnessed the first victory of Stanbury's Bess, a champion destined to become a legend.

Fifteen

As Zach watched horse and rider cross the finish line, his heart swelled inside his chest, though why that should be so he could not say. He had every reason to be angry with Judith—furiously angry for the risk she had taken—and no reason at all to feel such overwhelming pride in her accomplishment.

The filly had slowed her pace to a trot and was heading back to the paddock, with Judith all but standing in the stirrups, alternately waving to the cheering crowd and bending to pat the horse upon the neck. There was a look of such elation upon her face that Zach deeply regretted what he was about to do.

Judith had exhibited a skill and athletic ability that few men—and no women—could hope to attain. She had fought valiantly and won against opponents who possessed both more maturity and more experience than she. She had thrown her heart into the contest, risking all to do so, and she had triumphed. Gloriously! And now Zach must whisk her away before she could enjoy the accolades she had earned.

If he was to save her from the repercussions of her quixotic ride, he must remove her from the scene before anyone discovered her identity.

Never mind her valor, her spirit, or her brave heart; if

the gentlemen of the turf discovered that their newest hero was, in fact, a heroine, their adoration would quickly turn to condemnation. As for the less refined fans—especially those who had lost money as a result of Bess's victory—who could say what they might do? At the very least, the angry spectators would excoriate Judith, yelling contemptuous remarks and hurtful epithets. Her reputation would be in ruins. And not just her own. Her entire family would share in her disgrace.

There was only one way for Zach to protect her from such ignominy, and that was to take her from harm's way as quickly as possible.

Fortunately for his plan, a barrier was even now being wheeled into place to cordon off the winner's circle, for the officials had learned at previous races that they must aggressively stem the tide of bystanders, lest the well-wishers, in their enthusiasm, frighten or endanger the horse.

Also assisting in his plan were the two Rainsford grooms who stood just inside the paddock, ready to receive the new champion. Within the five minutes allowed for the assembling of the officials and dignitaries invited to the winner's circle for the presentation of the cup, the grooms would give Stanbury's Bess a quick toweling off, after which they would toss the new blanket upon her back, and lead her to the ceremony.

Zach checked one last time to make certain the bundle was still safely tied to his saddle. From his place behind the tall hedge, he waited until Judith and the filly were just outside the split-rail fence, then he signaled to Stan Rainsford, who in turn signaled to the grooms.

Continuing to play his part, Stan turned, offered his arm to Lilia as though he had nothing upon his mind but receiving his prize money, then proceeded toward the winner's circle. While the handsome young couple smiled and nodded to the well-wishers who lined the gravel walk, one of the grooms caught Bess's bridal and led her inside the paddock. Meanwhile, the other groom reached up and helped Judith from the horse, then he whispered something in her ear.

Zach watched, not daring to breathe, then as Judith nodded her head, he exhaled in relief. *Good girl! She meant to cooperate. No arguments. No questions.*

In a matter of moments, she and the servant were dashing to the far side of the paddock where he assisted her to climb up on the fence. She had just reached the top rail when Zach, astride the black gelding, trotted forward, stopping mere inches from where she sat, balanced and waiting.

Several onlookers had watched in puzzlement at the jockey's unusual behavior, but now they rushed forward, each wishing to have a share in the victory by touching the lucky winner. Realizing their intent, Zach hurriedly caught Judith around the waist and pulled her onto the horse in front of him.

" 'Ere now!" objected a fellow in a flashy yellow waistcoat. "Wot's this?"

"Gor blimey!" said another, his mouth hanging open, "the bloke's kidnapping the jockey."

As the muttering spectators pressed closer, Zach gave the gelding a nudge in the flank—a nudge that sent the horse surging forward, right through the middle of the crowd. While the irate fans jumped aside to avoid being trampled beneath the powerful hooves, Zach and Judith made good their escape.

"Have we a destination?" Judith asked.
"Now *that* sounds more like you."

They had sped from Blinbourne at a full gallop, not slowing their pace for at least five minutes, with Zach looking over his shoulder every so often to be certain no one followed them. Finally, satisfied that they had made a clean escape, he signaled the gelding to a trot.

"What sounds like me?"

"Wanting to know our destination. If memory serves me, you are the lady who said she preferred, whenever possible, to know where she was going. I believe you explained your position by stating that life had visited a number of surprises upon you lately, and that as a result, you liked to take charge of those few things still within your power."

Though his tone held a justifiable note of sarcasm, he chose not to quote her completely, a circumstance, Judith decided, that demonstrated a certain degree of forbearance on his part. She had, after all, finished that earlier remark by saying that *unlike him,* she did not like to gamble.

What irony! Had she not just risked her reputation? And upon a public horse race, of all things!

They said nothing more for a time, for Zach had turned the gelding off the main road onto a gently sloping green pasture. As they continued eastward, Judith spied the sheep path they had traversed Monday morning, and she knew they were headed back toward Gillmore House.

Not that she cared one whit where Zach was taking her. It was enough that Bess had won the race, and that Judith was safely away from the spectators—safely away from discovery. It was more than enough that she had been rescued by the man she loved, and that she was now in his arms.

Of course, she was not truly in his arms—not the way she would like to be—but for now it would have to do.

Taking advantage of the moment, Judith settled back

against Zach's chest, and to her delight, he tightened his hold on her waist, pulling her snugly against him. Happy with this latest development, she laid her head on his shoulder and closed her eyes, determined to enjoy her time with him, fearing that once he set her down, she might never see him again.

The clean, spicy fragrance of his shaving soap teased her nostrils, and she turned her face into his neck and breathed deeply, letting the scent of him fill her senses, savoring the aroma in much the same way she was relishing the feel of his strong, vibrant body close to hers. Breathing again, she wished this moment might last forever.

This has got to stop! Zach looked ahead, hoping their destination was in sight, for he was not at all certain how much more of this he could endure. After all, he was only human, and Judith was driving him to distraction. Though, in all honesty, he doubted she was aware of just how provocative she was being.

Not that he needed much provocation!

It was not enough that she was in his arms, her soft, yielding body pressed tantalizingly close against his. No. She had to be as near naked as made no difference. In breeches, no less. With her long, slender legs encased in revealing silk, and rubbing against his with every little movement.

Hoping to give his thoughts a different turn, he asked rather sharply, "Why did you do it? The race, I mean."

"I had to," she answered simply.

"And again I ask, why?"

"I could not let Stan be ruined. Not when Lilia's future is now inextricably joined with his. And of course," she added somewhat reluctantly, "there was the matter of your wager."

"My wager?" What was she talking about? The only

wager he had made was with her, and he had returned her locket a week ago.

"Your eight-hundred pounds," she said. "I could not let you lose it."

"What!"

Incredulous, Zach jerked the gelding to a stop, then he took Judith by the shoulders, turning her so he could look into her face. "Are you telling me you committed this mad, reckless act because you believed I had bet money upon the horse?"

"Why, yes," she said, those guileless doe's eyes looking up at him as though she had not the least idea why he was so angry with her.

Zach removed his hands from her shoulders, fearing he might be tempted to slip them up to her neck to throttle her. "Madam, what is this obsession you have with gambling?"

"I? It is you who are the gamester."

"So you have implied on more than one occasion. Though how you came to that conclusion I have yet to learn. Actually," he added, "I find most games boring in the extreme. Especially those where one sits for hours around a baize-covered table. As for testing my mettle, I find that real life, and the Exchange, do that quite thoroughly enough to suit me."

She stared at him, as though unable to credit what he had said. "The Exchange?"

He nodded.

"You mean, you are not . . ."

"Not," he agreed.

She seemed to require a few moments to assimilate this information. In time, however, her gamine's face broke into a smile of such unbelievable beauty that Zach was sorely tempted to end this discussion by taking her in his arms and kissing her senseless. Fortunately, he realized the folly of engaging in such an act while seated upon a horse, and gave the signal for the gelding to continue.

Within less than a minute they had arrived at their destination.

"It is the kissing gate," Judith said, when he reined in the gelding a second time. In some confusion, she glanced at the tall structure with its closely laid slat sides, then looked once again at Zach. "I assumed you were taking me to Gillmore House. Why have you brought me here?"

"For a little privacy."

Privacy?

Judith felt a blush warm her cheeks at the thought that he had brought her back to this spot, perhaps to continue what the shepherd had interrupted four days ago. When Zach dismounted then lifted her to the ground, his strong hands upon her waist, her heart very nearly leapt from her chest.

"I found your clothes on the floor of Bess's stall," he said, loosening the bundle that was tied to his saddle, "and I thought perhaps you could change inside the gate."

Judith's face grew even warmer than before. What a fool she was. She might have known Zachery Camden had not brought her here to kiss her!

He held the rolled bundle out to her. "I assumed you would not wish Lord Gillmore and the servants to see you in those carmine breeches, and the only enclosed place I could think of where you might change was the kissing gate."

"Of course," she said, taking the bundle. "I . . . I thank you, sir, for your foresight. It was very considerate of you to remember my situation."

"Your situation?"

"At Gillmore House," she replied.

Zach gave her his hand, assisting her in her descent from the rolling green pasture to the sheep track, then he turned his back to give her more privacy in the three-sided structure.

Getting right to the task for which she had come, Judith aligned the spindles so she could rotate them and go inside, choosing the farthest, and most sheltered, corner of the gate as the properest place to disrobe. While she tossed aside the jockey cap and cravat, then pulled the white silk shirt over her head, she was obliged to raise her voice to continue their conversation.

"With Lilia soon to be betrothed," she explained, "his lordship will be searching for some excuse to rid himself of my mother and me. And the earlier the better, I should imagine. That is why I thanked you, sir, for thinking of my clothes, for if Lord Gillmore should get wind of today's escapade, he would need to look no further."

Removing her shift from the bundle, she pulled the crumpled cambric over her head, then she smoothed it down over her hips and thighs before replacing the carmine breeches with her white lawn drawers. Eschewing the corset, she donned her green muslin frock and arranged the lace fichu across her bosom as neatly as possible.

As for her hair, which was coming loose from its topknot one lock at a time, there was nothing she could do to repair it without a looking glass. It was while she was rolling the corset inside the silks that Zach spoke again.

"Perhaps you will marry soon."

Startled by the sudden introduction of that most interesting topic, she asked, "What did you say?"

"Your situation," he replied, raising his voice. "Perhaps Miss Lilia will not be the only bride. You might even wed before her and quit Gillmore House at a time of your own choosing."

Judith grew perfectly still, not even daring to breathe. Though ladies discussed weddings and marriages with amazing regularity, gentlemen did not ordinarily bring up the subject. Not unless . . .

After swallowing the nerves that seemed suddenly to have leapt into her throat, constricting her vocal cords, Judith spoke slowly, choosing her words carefully. "Since no gentleman has made me the offer of his hand, nor even so much as declared that he feels some partiality for me, I . . . I cannot think it at all likely that I will wed before my sister."

When Zach said nothing more, Judith pressed her nose against the wooden sides of the gate, peering through the slats in an attempt to see him. As luck would have it, his back was still to her, so she could not read his face.

Hoping to get him to turn around, she said, "I shall probably never marry."

To her disappointment, the only response vouchsafed this observation was a strident *baa baa* from a sheep in the distant fold.

Taking the ovine commentary in bad part, Judith raised her voice almost to shouting level. "Not that I have turned my face against the wedded state, you understand. It is just that I have no portion to bring to the union, nor have I Lilia's beauty to offset the deficit."

Zach muttered something that sounded like, "Absolute lunacy."

"I beg your pardon," she said, her heart beating a double-time cadence in her ears, "I did not quite hear that last."

"I said you are the most beautiful woman I have ever known."

"I am?"

"You are. And any man fortunate enough to win your love would be the richest man in the world."

In her haste to exit the gate, Judith stepped upon the discarded silks, her thoughts focused on nothing but aligning the spindles and shoving them forward. Once she was outside, she stopped just behind Zach and tapped him on the shoulder.

He turned and looked at her for a long, nerve-racking moment, those cool gray eyes more serious than she had ever seen them before. Then he smiled, and in an instant, all those feelings Judith had dispatched to distant regions of her heart rose in her in one joyous, triumphant wave, almost drowning her in happiness.

Overwhelmed by the intensity of her emotions, she asked nothing more of life than to be allowed to throw herself into Zach's arms and kiss him to her heart's content.

But she dare not do that. Not yet.

"Zach," she said, "before I make a complete fool of myself, I need to hear the words from your own lips. Are you, or are you not, proposing to me?"

"Wood nymph," he said, the softness of his voice reaching inside Judith and squeezing the very breath from her lungs, "I am very much afraid I am."

"Afraid?"

"Petrified, actually. Just as you should be, for I warn you, I have not your warm heart, nor your loving nature. If you choose to join your future with mine, you will be taking a chance. A real gamble."

Judith stepped very close to him "I can learn to be a gambler."

Apparently pleased to hear it, Zach slipped his arms around her waist and pulled her close against him—gratifyingly close—and though he seemed thoroughly absorbed in observing her lips, he still did not offer to kiss her.

Zach knew she wanted to be kissed. He could see it in her eyes, and Heaven help him, he wanted to oblige her.

Wanted it desperately! With Judith in his arms, her lovely face turned up to his, it was all he could do to control the desire that burned inside him. He yearned to taste her soft, tempting lips, to cover her mouth with his own, and experience once again her innocent, uninhibited response.

But he dare not give in to that yearning.

He had just extricated her from one threat to her reputation, he could not ignore this newest danger. If someone should see them kissing, there would be no explaining the truth of the situation. And in all fairness to those hypothetical scandalmongers, Judith looked as though she had just come from a tumble in the haystack.

She would be mortified if she knew it, of course, but anyone seeing her at the moment could be forgiven for thinking the worst. Her hair was mussed and beginning to fall about her neck and shoulders; her clothing was wrinkled and had been donned in apparent haste; and to add the final piece of incriminating evidence, tell-tale straw adhered to the skirt of her green muslin frock.

No, he dare not kiss her, and wanting to turn her thoughts from amorous pursuits, Zach said the first thing that occurred to him. "I should have known this would happen."

"Should you?" she asked.

"Definitely, for there is something in the Dorset air. Something that makes all the men impatient to find themselves a wife. Whatever that strange power may be, even the very young are not immune to it, for Master Jeremy Wimmer informed me that he, too, wishes to be wed."

The moment he uttered the words, Zach knew he had made a tactical error. From the sudden mischievous light in Judith's eyes, something about Master Wimmer had put an idea into the minx's head.

"Ohh!" she moaned, grasping her left wrist with her right hand. "Ohhhhh!"

Though not fooled in the least by her attempt at theatrics, Zach said, "My dear girl, what is wrong?"

"I am injured," she said, adding a rather pathetic note to her voice.

"You poor creature. It was the race, no doubt."

Her sigh was worthy of the great Mrs. Siddons. "I should not have done it," she replied, "for I fear I have sustained a bruise or two."

Zach loosened his grip upon her waist, though he made no attempt to move away. "Perhaps I should ride for the apothecary."

"No, no!" she said, pushing his arms back securely around her. "I thought *you* might do something to soothe the pain."

Despite his resolve, Zach felt the corners of his lips twitch. "Liniment, perhaps?"

"Actually, I had in mind that other therapy you mentioned."

"Other therapy?"

"You remember," she said, tipping her head a bit to the side, and looking at him in a way that very nearly convinced him to give up the game and crush her to him. "You mentioned the palliative when I was at Wimmer Cottage. A regimen practiced by a nursemaid, I believe you said."

"Ah, yes. You mean the *kiss-it-to-make-it-better* therapy."

"The very thing!" she said.

Her smile was like the sun's rays after a storm, and Zach found himself a converted sun worshiper. Giving in to the incvitable, he lifted her hand to his lips, then he turned her wrist so the vulnerable inside was exposed, and placed a kiss upon the soft skin.

"Ummm," she said.

"Better?"

"Much. At least, it is better in my wrist. Oddly, the pain seems to have moved farther up my arm."

Not at all surprised by this medical anomaly, Zach applied his personal curative to the satiny skin just inside her elbow.

For a moment Judith was quiet, her eyes closed, as if enjoying the feel of his lips upon her skin, then she began to moan again. "Ooh! Ooh!"

"What now?" he asked, his voice not nearly as annoyed as his words might indicate.

"It is my shoulder. The throbbing is quite unbearable. I declare, I do not know how I am to tolerate such discomfort."

"Madam, you are a martyr."

She sighed. "If only I might prevail upon you to try what you could to relieve my suffering."

"Of course. How can I refuse?"

He pushed the fichu aside an inch and bent to touch his lips to her exposed shoulder. While he was thus, with his thick, black hair so close to her face, Judith was unable to resist the temptation to touch the crisp strands. Fortunately, Zach's was a forbearing nature, and he remained still, allowing her probing fingers to roam where they would.

Some time later, he raised his head and looked into her eyes, and when he spoke, his voice was noticeably husky. "How is your mouth, my love?"

"It . . . it definitely needs attention."

"What would you have me do?" he asked, drawing her willing body even closer.

Winding her arms around his neck, she bid him practice his healing art. "Please," she begged, "put me out of my misery."

More than happy to oblige, Zach bent and covered her mouth with his own.

WATCH FOR THESE ZEBRA REGENCIES

LADY STEPHANIE   (0-8217-5341-X, $4.50)
by Jeanne Savery
Lady Stephanie Morris has only one true love: the family estate she
has managed ever since her mother died. But then Lord Anthony Rider
arrives on her estate, claiming he has plans for both the land and the
woman. Stephanie soon realizes she's fallen in love with a man whose
sensual caresses will plunge her into a world of peril and intrigue . . . a
man as dangerous as he is irresistible.

BRIGHTON BEAUTY   (0-8217-5340-1, $4.50)
by Marilyn Clay
Chelsea Grant, pretty and poor, naively takes school friend Alayna
Marchmont's place and spends a month in the country. The devastating
man had sailed from Honduras to claim his promised bride, Miss
Marchmont. An affair of the heart may lead to disaster . . . unless a
resourceful Brighton beauty finds a way to stop a masquerade and
keep a lord's love.

LORD DIABLO'S DEMISE   (0-8217-5338-X, $4.50)
by Meg-Lynn Roberts
The sinfully handsome Lord Harry Glendower was a gambler and the
black sheep of his family. About to be forced into a marriage of con-
venience, the devilish fellow engineered his own demise, never having
dreamed that faking his death would lead him to the heavenly refuge
of spirited heiress Gwyn Morgan, the daughter of a physician.

A PERILOUS ATTRACTION   (0-8217-5339-8, $4.50)
by Dawn Aldridge Poore
Alissa Morgan is stunned when a frantic passenger thrusts her baby
into Alissa's arms and flees, having heard rumors that a notorious
highwayman posed a threat to their coach. Handsome stranger Hugh
Sebastian secretly possesses the treasured necklace the highwayman
seeks and volunteers to pose as Alissa's husband to save her reputation.
With a lost baby and missing necklace in their care, the couple embarks
on a journey into peril—and passion.

*Available wherever paperbacks are sold, or order direct from the
Publisher. Send cover price plus 50¢ per copy for mailing and
handling to Penguin USA, P.O. Box 999, c/o Dept. 17109,
Bergenfield, NJ 07621. Residents of New York and Tennessee must
include sales tax. DO NOT SEND CASH.*